THE WITCH OF
BEN HILL COUNTY

THE WITCH OF
BEN HILL COUNTY

JACLYN WELDON WHITE

DEEDS PUBLISHING

Published by Deeds Publishing in Athens, GA
www.deedspublishing.com

Printed in The United States of America

Cover design and text layout by Mark Babcock

Library of Congress Cataloging-in-Publications data is available upon request.

ISBN 978-1-947309-07-4

Books are available in quantity for promotional or premium use. For information, email info@deedspublishing.com.

First Edition, 2017

10 9 8 7 6 5 4 3 2 1

PROLOGUE

THE WITCH ALWAYS OPENED HER DOOR BEFORE YOU COULD knock on it. The girl was sure she hadn't made any noise walking down the dirt road to the little house, so she figured it had to be magic.

"I . . . I know it's late, but I just had to —"

"Come on in, honey. Don't you worry about that." The old woman looked like she was ready for bed. A shapeless old night-gown hung from her shoulders and white hair trailed down her back. But she smiled and opened the door wider. "Sit by the fire, child. You look chilled."

The girl stepped into the dim room and took a seat in an old rocking chair. The damp night air had cut right through her denim jacket and the warmth was welcome.

"Want a cup of tea?"

"No, ma'am."

"How's your mama? Does she need some more of that salve?"

"No, she's fine. I . . . I came for me this time." She took a deep breath. "I need one of your spells, a protection spell, I guess you'd call it."

A black cat rubbed against her legs on its way to stretch out on the hearth. The witch looked her up and down.

"You've got trouble, don't you? Are you in a family way, child?"

The girl nodded.

"Is it the same man we've talked about before?"

"Yessum, but that's not why I came."

"He's no good for you. You know that."

"I know, but that's not a problem," she said. "Not now. Me and this baby'll be just fine. He's gonna take care of us. I know that."

"He'll never leave his wife."

The girl looked down, uneasy under the witch's penetrating gaze. "No, ma'am. I guess I know he won't do that. But he'll do what's right for me and this baby. He won't have a choice."

The old woman sighed. "I wish I believed he would, but that man has never done the right thing in his whole sorry life. Not much chance he's going to start now."

The girl's smile was a combination of guile and certainty. "I guarantee he will this time, 'cause I've got something he'll do anything to keep people from knowing, proof that he ..." She shook her head. "All I'm saying is he'll take care of me, 'cause if he doesn't, it'll be real bad for him."

The fire popped twice, loud in the quiet room, and the witch frowned. "I've told you before that your happiness isn't linked to that man. Bad luck and sorrow and death walk with him. You need to look somewhere else for your future."

"Really, everything's going to be fine. I know it is."

The witch's eyes narrowed. "If you're so sure about that, why do you think you need protection?"

The girl took a deep breath. "Well, it couldn't hurt now, could it? It's not just him, you know. I'm gonna have a baby to worry about. Lots of stuff can go wrong with babies, everybody knows that. You can't have too much protection."

The naiveté of the young could break your heart. The witch sighed, got slowly to her feet and crossed to her work table where baskets of dried herbs sat beside several blue and brown bottles.

A sudden gust of wind rattled the branches of the trees outside the little house and the girl shivered. This part, when the witch concocted her charms, always gave her a creepy feeling, like something awful might jump out of one of those baskets.

"I'll make you up a little something," the witch said, choosing several leaves from the baskets and dropping them into a tiny red velvet bag, "but nothing can protect you from evil, child." From a cobalt bottle, she took a pinch of what looked like black salt and added that to the bag as well. "And that man, he's pure evil."

She closed the bag with a ribbon drawstring and bowed her head in a quick prayer. Then she handed it to the girl. "Carry this with you—all the time. It'll help keep you and your baby safe, but only if you get away from *him*. Nothing can help you if you stay."

The witch stood at her door and watched as the girl walked back up the road. The moon was so bright that she could see the small figure for a good while. A night bird screamed in the distance and the witch shivered. She knew there were no spells strong enough to protect that girl.

ONE

CATHERINE CLOONEY WAS DEAD. I WAS SORRY, BUT NOT heartbroken. After all, I'd only known her for six months and she'd lived a good 92 years. We'd been friendly, but not what you'd call intimate. So, I was more than a little surprised to be waiting to meet with her lawyer that November morning.

Perched on the nineteenth floor of a sleek Atlanta skyscraper, the office was a quiet place, tastefully and expensively furnished. The elegant receptionist matched her surroundings. She had taken my name and notified someone by phone that I was there, then gone back to her keyboard without giving me another glance.

At precisely 10:00, a young woman appeared through a doorway and ushered me into Arthur J. Trotmyer's office. It was all plush carpet and dark wood, with a shiny new set of law books lining the built-in shelves. Trotmyer himself was almost as new as the books. With his carefully styled hair, discreet pin-striped suit and pale gray tie, he looked like an eager college freshman, all dressed up, pretending to be a lawyer. I realized he must be a very junior member of the firm. He rose when I entered and came around the desk to shake my hand and guide me to a chair.

"Mrs. Christopher?" He was clean-shaven and smiling. "So glad to meet you. I'm Arthur Trotmyer."

"Nice to meet you, Mr. Trotmyer." I'd have bet a bundle that his mother called him Artie.

"Please make yourself comfortable."

There was a faint, strangled cry from the room next door and I wondered what hardship had brought that poor soul to a law office.

Trotmyer resumed his seat behind the desk. Its shiny wooden surface was bare except for two pens and a single manila folder. "Would you like coffee or maybe a nice cup of tea, dear?"

Dear. I swallowed my irritation at the affectionate term. One of the disadvantages of passing fifty is that any number of people — from waitresses and salespersons to upstart lawyers — feel free to address you in terms of endearment. I could have said a lot on the topic, but Trotmyer wasn't important enough for the effort. I just wanted to get this over with.

"Nothing, thank you."

He opened the folder, glanced briefly at the top page, then smiled at me again. "I suppose you know why I asked you here."

"I really don't, Mr. Trotmyer. I got your letter, of course, but I can't imagine why Catherine would mention me in her will."

He nodded. "People are often surprised. Still, you and Mrs. Clooney must have been very close."

"Not really. We were neighbors, but not close friends."

"That's right. You lived near her in that retirement community, didn't you?"

"Active adult," I corrected automatically.

"Hmmm?"

"Active adult. It's an active adult community — for people 55 and over." I could see he had no idea what I was talking about. For some reason, most people think that living in an over-55 community means you've taken up residence in a nursing home. I decided not to try to explain it to him.

"Oh, yes, yes, of course. What's it called again?"

"Marchpoint Manse."

"Of course. Unusual name, isn't it?"

"Very." I don't have any idea where Marchpoint came from and I never understood the Manse part myself. It means clergyman's house—I looked it up to be sure—and doesn't make much sense when used to describe a 1,200-home subdivision.

"Catherine lived there for several years. I moved in across the street from her in April. Like I said, we were neighbors. We had coffee together a few times. Once or twice I took her to the doctor when her daughter couldn't, but I wouldn't say we were close."

He frowned. "I see. Well, she certainly must have trusted you. Let me just read from the document itself." He cleared his throat importantly. "It's paragraph eight. There are two clauses. Yes, here it is. 'To my dear friend Emily Christopher, I leave the continuing care of my beloved cat Curtis, knowing she will care for and love him as I do. To cover the cost of his food and upkeep, I also bequeath to her the sum of $2,000.'"

There was another wail from next door and this time I thought I knew the source. If I hadn't been afraid of losing my dignity, I'd have howled right along with him.

"She left me her *cat*?" Catherine's sweet, smiling face flashed in my memory and I wondered how someone who'd seemed so kind could have done something this treacherous.

"That's right, dear," he said, beaming. All was fine in Arthur J. Trotmyer's world. "And a very generous allowance for his care, too."

"But I don't want a cat. I've never had pets. Never wanted them.

7

Besides, I work odd hours. Sometimes I'm gone for days at a time."
I took a deep breath. "I don't know anything about taking care of an
animal. Surely there's somebody else who'd be better at this."

Trotmyer was frowning as if he thought I was a poor choice for
the job, but he sat up a bit straighter, squared his shoulders and
plowed ahead. "From what I understand, cats are quite content being left alone. They're rather aloof animals, aren't they?"

Another howl could be heard through the wall. It didn't aloof;
it sounded really angry.

"And Mrs. Clooney very thoughtfully left several pages of instructions about the cat's care, along with copies of all his medical
records."

She kept *all* his medical records? Hell, I couldn't lay hands on all
my *own* medical records. I was impressed, but not swayed.

"Mr. Trotmyer, I really can't take him. Isn't there somebody else?"

He shook his head. "Sadly, no. When I drew up the will for Mrs.
Clooney, I anticipated we might encounter a problem with this item.
I asked her then if there were someone we could add as a contingent
heir — in case you were unable to take Curtis. But she had only the
one daughter, who's in her 70s, and is unfortunately allergic to cats.

"Mrs. Clooney was sure you'd be willing to take on the respon-
sibility." He sighed. "However, if you won't, you won't. I certainly
can't compel you to accept the bequest." He began straightening the
papers in the folder. "I suppose the poor animal will have to be sent
to the local shelter. He might even be adopted, although I understand that's unlikely for adult cats."

That was a nasty card to play. Part of me didn't really believe
Trotmyer would condemn the cat to that fate, but he looked serious
about it and I couldn't take the chance. "Oh, okay. I'll take him."

"Wonderful!" He was Mr. Congeniality again.

"Wait. I'll take him, but only with the understanding that, if it doesn't work out, I can find him another home and transfer the money to his new owner."

"You can do whatever you like, Mrs. Christopher, once you've taken possession of the animal. Mrs. Clooney placed no restrictions on that." He picked up the will again. "Now shall we proceed to the second clause?"

"Why not?" What more could Catherine do to me from the grave?

He cleared his throat again. "This is more in the form of a request than an outright bequest. I'll just read it, if I may. 'It is my wish that Emily Christopher use her knowledge and experience to investigate the theft of $8,000 from my great-grandson Daniel Cooper and his wife Stacy. While the official conclusion was that nothing illegal took place, I am convinced that a theft occurred. I request that Emily look into the matter and do what she can to remedy the situation. To help her accomplish that, I instruct that she be given $2,000.' He looked up. "That's it."

He seemed to be waiting for me to comment, but I didn't have anything to say. What had Catherine been *thinking*?

"Mrs. Clooney left a packet of information for you which, I presume, includes the details of the situation with her great-grandson."

"Why on earth would Catherine think I could help with something like that?"

"I understood that you are employed in the field of law enforcement."

"Well, yeah, I was with the police department for a number of years and then worked as an investigator with the DA's Office.

But I'm ... I guess you'd call it semi-retired. These days I work part time as a consultant for the DA's Office, usually trial preparation." I leaned forward in my chair. "Mr. Trotmyer, I've never worked for an individual. If Catherine had $4,000 to throw around, why didn't she just send the money to her great-grandson? And give him the cat, too. He'd have half his money back that way."

His face was stiff with disapproval. "I counseled with Mrs. Clooney about this. She believed there was a principle at stake here."

I sighed. God save us from people who do things for the principle at stake.

"She wanted to ensure that the man who stole this money would be brought to justice. And, melodramatic as it sounds, she honestly believed that, if it didn't happen, her great-grandson might do something drastic—hurt or even kill the man. The boy has a temper and has evidently made some threats to that effect."

"Then why not leave the money to his parents? Let them hire a private detective or someone to work on it?"

"Both his parents are deceased. A traffic accident several years ago," he said. "I thought you would have known that. Catherine's only family were her daughter and this great-grandson. He and his family live in Fitzgerald, in south Georgia."

I tried one more time. "I'm sorry to hear that, but how am *I* supposed to fix this if the 'official conclusion' is that nothing illegal happened?"

He just shook his head and I smothered an impulse to slap that perfectly shaved cheek. A headache was building at the base of my skull. "Well, what if I just refuse to do anything? Can you send the money to her great-grandson instead?"

"No, there's no provision for that. As you heard, there's only the request and the instruction that you be given a sum of money. There are no requirements to be met nor are there any results that must be achieved. If you're so inclined, you may certainly send all or part of the money to Mr. Cooper. Or you may simply take the money and disregard her request for help."

"I see."

His young face creased in a middle-aged frown. "Very unwise, the whole thing. I didn't approve of such a bequest being made without some provision for accountability, but Mrs. Clooney insisted it be done this way. She told me you were one of the most trustworthy people she'd ever met." He clearly didn't share Catherine's opinion. He got to his feet. "At least it's out of my hands now. I'll just instruct my secretary to bring your check and I'll go fetch Curtis."

Ten minutes later, I was on an elevator with a $4,000 check and a cat named Curtis in a wire and plastic carrier. The cat began the trip with a couple of growls and an evil hiss, but as the car descended, he grew more and more vocal. His deep growls escalated into chilling howls, the sort of sounds you'd expect from the minor demons of hell.

My fellow passengers moved as far away from me as the small space allowed, and I hoped the carrier was a sturdy one. If he got loose in that elevator, Curtis could shred us all to ribbons by the time we reached the lobby.

TWO

THE TRIP FROM DOWNTOWN ATLANTA TO BLOUNT COUNTY, A suburban area some 40 miles northeast of the city, usually takes an hour or a little more unless you're foolish enough to attempt it during rush hours. That Tuesday morning, with no incidents and comparatively light traffic, I made the drive in only 50 minutes, but it seemed much, much longer. Curtis squalled every minute of every mile. He soon found his rhythm. Howl, howl, howl, inhale. Howl, howl, howl, inhale. And he never stopped.

When we finally reached the gated entrance to Marchpoint Manse, I veered into the resident lane where a touch on the clicker lifted the gate and allowed me to drive through.

I made three more turns, waving at several walkers—with and without dogs—then pulled into my driveway.

"We're home!" I told my captive. He paid no attention, just continued to complain.

I hauled the carrier into the house, a task made more difficult by the cat pacing back and forth, constantly changing the center of balance. It was a relief to set it down on the kitchen floor. I unlatched the mesh door and let it fall open, then braced for the worst. It was almost a letdown when Curtis exited the carrier slowly and cautiously, each step deliberate and considered. He surveyed the kitchen around him, then saw me and gave a devilish hiss.

He didn't look like a demon—a gray tabby with long legs and goldish green eyes which, at the moment, were taking in this new territory. I knew he'd probably had a bad few weeks since Catherine's death, in strange places with strange people, and I actually felt a little sorry for him.

"It's going to be okay, buddy." I crossed to the refrigerator and opened the door. "How about a nice bowl of milk?"

I turned around with the milk jug and a reassuring smile, but Curtis had left the kitchen. I went to see where he'd gone, but he was nowhere in sight.

"Come on, cat," I said, looking in the hall bath and my office. "Don't make this any harder than it has to be. I don't have time for hide and seek."

I finally found him crouched in a living room corner behind an oversized potted plant. Neither milk, sweet talk, nor even tuna could coax him out. When I tried to pet him, he hissed again and retreated farther back in the corner. Evidently that was where he planned to stay for a while.

I went and sat at the kitchen table where I could look out over the small front lawn—turning brown now that winter was approaching—and the quiet street beyond. What was I going to do with a cat, especially one that hated me? Why on earth did Catherine believe I should take him? And why should I keep him? I didn't owe her a thing, did I?

That triggered a twinge of guilt. Catherine had never made demands on me before. In fact, she'd gone out of her way to be kind. When a power surge knocked out my electricity a month after I moved in, she helped me move all the food from my freezer into hers so it wouldn't spoil. She never minded picking up my mail when I was out of town and she brought me soup and cold drinks and checked on me several times a day after the flu knocked me flat back in early June. So, okay, maybe I did owe her—a little.

Trotmyer's manila envelope was on the table in front of me. Putting it off wouldn't make it any better. The first thing I pulled out was a sheaf of stapled papers. Glimpsing the words *hairball treatment* left no doubt as to what these were. I skipped Curtis's medical history and turned to the instructions for his care. The whole process seemed unnecessarily complicated, but I realized there were a few items I was going to have to have right away. A shopping trip was in order.

The rest of the envelope's contents related to Catherine's great-grandson and his troubles. There were court documents, newspaper clippings and a three-page, typewritten letter from Catherine.

When I finished the letter, I understood why she wanted justice. What happened to Danny and Stacy Cooper was shameful. It was unethical and mean, but, from what I could see, not illegal. I had no idea how anything I might do could help them.

The big box pet supply place was unfamiliar territory for me. Wandering up and down the aisles—who knew there were so many products for so many different kinds of pets?—I loaded my cart with a litter box and the litter to go in it, a puffy green cat bed, and a bag of the dry food Catherine's notes indicated Curtis liked. On impulse, I added a couple of bags of cat treats and a catnip-filled toy mouse. At check out, I shelled out more money than I'd expected.

"Do you need some help getting that out to your car, hon?" the fortyish woman at the register asked.

I gritted my teeth. "I think I can manage, *hon.*"

I did. And in spite of my advanced age and feeble condition, I was even able to drive myself home.

I was pulling my purchases out of the back of the Trailblazer when Linda Winkler glided silently into my driveway at the wheel of a bright green golf cart. Golf carts are a favorite mode of transportation in Marchpoint.

If you didn't look close enough to see the faint lines on her face, you might mistake Linda for a young woman. In jeans and a tie-dyed poncho, she was reed thin, barely topped five feet, and still retained a lot of the waif-like quality she'd had as a teenager. She'd worn her hair in the same style since the seventies—long and straight, and parted in the middle with deep bangs. Now it was brown and silver gray instead of sun-streaked blond, but the effect was the same.

We'd met in the ninth grade and been friends for over forty years. Linda was the reason I'd moved to Marchpoint. She'd lived in the neighborhood for two years, moving in soon after her husband Mark died. It was her glowing description of the place that caused me to check it out.

"What have you got there?" She hopped out of the cart. "Is that—no. Surely you didn't get a *cat*?"

I explained Catherine's will and my bequest as I lugged the food and litter box into the house. Linda picked up the bag of litter and followed. She dropped it with a thud and looked around.

"So, where is it?"

"The cat? Last I saw, he was hiding behind that big plant in the living room."

She went to look. "Yeah, here he is."

"Be careful," I advised, coming into the room. "He's not very friendly."

"Oh, he's just scared is all." She squatted down and spoke in what I assumed was a cat-friendly voice. "Hey, there, sweet thing. Aren't you a pretty cat? Will you let me pet you? Oh, sure you will. You're just a little nervous. I'll just scratch you behind your — Owww!"

When she drew back her hand, blood was springing from a scratch across two knuckles. "Guess he didn't want to be petted after all."

THREE

I SMEARED ANTIBIOTIC CREAM ON THE CUTS AND COVERED them with bandages while I told Linda about Catherine's other request and how her great-grandson had been swindled out of his money.

"It was a real estate scam, just barely legal, but I don't see anything I can do about it."

"There must be *something*." I wasn't surprised that she sounded distressed. Linda was the most kind-hearted person I'd ever met. "I mean, think of those poor kids, saving their money and dreaming about a house, and then getting ripped off. That man just killed their dreams!"

I shook my head. "There just isn't anything…"

Her big blue eyes widened beseechingly under her shaggy bangs.

I sighed. "Look, I'll think about it some more. Maybe there's something I've overlooked. You want a cup of coffee?"

"Thanks, no. I can't stay." She ran a hand through her hair. "I've got yoga at the clubhouse in half an hour." She sighed in mock exhaustion. "This is a really busy week for me. Tomorrow morning is my dream therapy class at the arts center over in Reddingtton and then I'm doing a Reiki session at four."

I opened the pantry and found a place for the cat treats. "Mico and Eben and Annette are coming over to watch the game Saturday night. Why don't you join us?"

"Oh, I'd love to — it's been ages since I've seen Mico — but I can't. Bobby's birthday is that night. I'll be there for the cake and candles, but it'll have to be an early night 'cause the contemplative nature walk is at 7:00 Sunday morning. Oh, and I'm teaching past life exploration that afternoon."

Linda could toss out statements like "past life exploration" as casually as if she were talking about grocery shopping. She'd always been a lot more out there than I was. Within an hour of our first meeting in freshman biology class, she announced she had The Sight. Her grandmother had it, she confided, which was how she'd gotten it. I thought it sounded like a hereditary disease, but Linda was proud of what she considered her birthright.

I remembered her telling me about her dreams, pronouncing them visions, and later, when they came true, claiming that proved she was psychic. Since a lot of the things she told me were going to happen weren't exactly unexpected, like me flunking an algebra test, I never put a lot of stock in her predictions.

Unlike Linda, I've always seen the world in stark black and white. Even back in the seventies, with the remnants of the Age of Aquarius all around me, I wasn't inclined to put stock in anything I couldn't see with my own eyes. And I wasn't shy about sharing that belief with my friend.

But my skepticism never interfered with our friendship. While Linda found more receptive people with which to share her visions and theories, we still spent a lot of time together. Our activities and conversations usually centered on the more mundane aspects of our lives. In high school and college, it was boys and grades and ambitions. As we aged, we focused more on family and work. But in all those years, a week rarely passed without our speaking.

Linda still occasionally cautioned me about something or someone. The last direct warning I remembered came a few years back when she told me to beware of traitorous friends. Later I figured she must have heard rumors about my adulterous husband and was trying to give me a tactful heads-up.

Linda's fascination with mysticism had dwindled some over the years as marriage and motherhood required more and more of her, but she'd returned to it with a vengeance since Mark's death. In fact, she seemed determined to explore every alternative philosophy she could find. She'd taken up the tarot, casting runes, reading tea leaves, angel readings, and probably twenty more things I didn't even know about.

A year ago, she opened a little vitamin and book store in a nearby strip mall. There, along with herbs and vitamins and the usual bestsellers, she sold books on spiritualism, astrology, ghosts, and any other sort of mystical things you could imagine. After hours, she hosted New Age classes.

"Well, I wouldn't expect you to miss your only son's birthday. Sounds like you'll be running all weekend."

"I absolutely will." A frown crossed her pretty face. "Oh, yeah, I wanted to let you know there were a couple more robberies yesterday. And last night I heard something outside my back door." She shivered. "I was too scared to look, but I think it might have been somebody trying to get in."

Linda thought she heard intruders at least once a week and a hang-up phone call sent her into a panic, sure that thieves were casing her home.

"It was probably the wind," I suggested. Marchpoint was built around several tracts of wooded acreage, crisscrossed by wide nature trails. "Or a raccoon or possum. You know there's a lot of wildlife through here at night."

"Maybe so ..." She wasn't convinced.

I twisted the top off the plastic jug of cat litter. "So, what kind of thefts did we have yesterday? Anything new?"

"I don't guess so," she said reluctantly. "The same kind of stuff that's been happening since last year. Clarice Mock left her purse on the kitchen table while she was having coffee at Val Peters' house. Just across the street, you know? When she got back, her wallet was laying on the floor and she was missing about $50."

I didn't have to ask how the thief got in. Marchpointers were bad about leaving doors unlocked, a result of the false sense of security that comes from living in a gated community. "Anything else taken? Credit cards? Jewelry?"

"No, just the cash. And Walt Simmons, you know him, don't you? He organizes the bocce league? Well, anyhow, somebody took a little yard ornament from his garage. One of those cute ceramic garden sculptures—a rabbit with a top hat."

"What was it doing in the garage if it was a yard ornament?"

She shrugged. "I guess they hadn't decided where they could put it so that the HOA would approve."

The Marchpoint Homeowners Association was run by a vigilant committee that rarely missed opportunities to advise homeowners they'd violated neighborhood covenants. The rules declared that no statuary or any other form of ornamentation could be displayed in yards if it was visible from the street. The result was block after block of plain-looking houses with remarkably decorative backyards.

"Well, that doesn't sound too serious," I told her. I poured some of the litter into the plastic litter box, then stepped back from the cloud of dust rising above it. "I doubt if we have gangs of burglars cruising the neighborhood. They'd have a hard time getting through the gate in a car and, if they climbed one of the fences, they wouldn't be able to steal anything they couldn't carry out in their hands. It's probably somebody's visiting grandchildren."

I'd spent four of my twelve years with the county police department as a burglary detective and knew that a good percentage of residential burglaries were committed by kids looking for quick cash and excitement.

"I guess it could have been kids," she said doubtfully.

I opened the cat food, poured half a cup or so into a cereal bowl and set it on the floor near the kitchen bookcase. I filled a second bowl with water and placed it beside the first.

Linda was moving toward the back door, then stopped with her hand on the handle. "Oh, one more thing," she said with a nonchalant air that didn't fool me for a second. "Guess who came in the shop yesterday?"

"Who?"

"Owen," she lowered her voice as if she might be overheard gossiping right there in my kitchen, "buying male potency capsules—they're called male enhancement aids. I don't think he noticed me until he brought them up to the cash register and saw me. For a minute, I thought he was going to run right out the door."

We both broke into peals of laughter, picturing my ex-husband's discomfort.

"Oh," I said when I could speak again, "oh, I wish I could have seen that. I bet he wanted to crawl under a rock!"

"Yep, that's just how he looked. But I was very professional, didn't say a word about what he was buying. Just rang 'em up and put 'em in a bag for him." She tilted her head to one side. "Maybe that's why he stayed to chat a minute. He... ummm... told me he and Sarah were moving in here."

I wasn't prepared for the burn of fury that shot through me. "You mean in *Marchpoint*?"

"Yeah, he seemed real excited about it." She bit her lip. "I can't believe they'd want to move here with you already... I mean it just seems like it would be so awkward. But, anyway, he said they've been looking at those big houses over in the Arbor. He said Sarah just fell in love with one on Blackberry Ridge."

I tried to absorb this news without an outward show of anger. Marchpoint Manse was divided into three sections. The houses in the Village, where Linda and I lived, were the smallest and least expensive—most were two bedrooms and two baths, with a study or office. Homes in the Meadows had three bedrooms and larger living spaces. The Arbor boasted the biggest houses, complete with basements, huge kitchens, formal dining rooms and four or five bedrooms. The houses there cost twice what my little place did.

I wasn't surprised they'd chosen the Arbor. Owen always had liked showy things and he could afford them. He was an extremely successful attorney and considered to be an all-around great guy. I'd thought so, too, until about five years ago when I caught him in our bed with my then dear friend Sarah Candler.

Linda was looking a bit uneasy. "I hate being the one to tell you, but I knew you'd rather hear it from me. I mean, it'd be awful if you didn't know and just ran into Owen or Sarah in the gym or saw her power walking around the neighborhood. I remember how much that woman loves to exercise."

She always had. It was how Sarah kept her pampered, home-wrecking body battle-ready.

I squeezed Linda's arm affectionately. "Thanks for telling me. You probably saved me from a nasty surprise."

I followed Linda back outside. A brisk November wind had started and kept her poncho shifting around her in a swirl of color. Even though the sun was bright, that wind prevented the day from feeling really warm. As Linda climbed into her cart, a roar shook the air. Conversation had to stop as a big black motorcycle passed the house and glided smoothly up the driveway of the house across the street. The garage door rose and the motorcycle entered and came to a stop beside a shiny red car. A moment later, the engine was switched off and quiet returned.

We watched as a man, dressed from shoulder to toe in black leather, stepped off the machine and removed his helmet. At that distance, it was hard to tell any more about him than he was tall, fit, and had longish graying hair. Then the garage door slid back down, cutting off our view.

"My goodness," Linda said. "So that's your new neighbor, huh? Quite a change from Catherine."

"You could say that. The most noise Catherine ever caused around here was rolling her garbage can out to the curb." I shook my head. "This guy doesn't mind bothering everyone whenever he comes and goes."

"Oh, it wasn't so bad," Linda said. "And it's a beautiful bike. Kinda reminds me of the one Mark had."

"It's a nice one, I guess." I knew she had fond memories of biking trips with her husband and didn't want to sound disapproving, but I couldn't believe a motorcycle had to be so *loud*. You'd think the HOA would do something about *that* instead of worrying about rabbit statues.

After Linda left, I fetched the mail. As usual, it was mostly junk, advertising hearing aids, retirement plans, and medical offices. That was one of the drawbacks to living in an over-55 community.

Back in the house, Curtis was still in hiding. I fixed myself a cup of tea and thought about Owen and Sarah. How could they do something so tacky? The idea of their moving into my neighborhood gave me the same feeling you get when you discover a fly in your mashed potatoes, but worrying about it wouldn't change things. I took a deep breath and told myself I could rise above this.

Although I couldn't erase the knowledge that they were coming to Marchpoint, I forced myself to stop dwelling on it. My energy needed to be directed at setting up the house to accommodate a cat.

FOUR

I PUT THE LITTER BOX IN THE HALL BATHROOM AND TRIED
again to lure Curtis out from behind the plant, but he wouldn't
budge. He simply ignored me. I ignored him right back. For the
next couple of hours I settled in the office and finished some work
for the DA's Office. It wasn't hard—just vetting a couple of witnesses for an upcoming trial. There was nothing questionable in either
one's background and it only took a short while to write a report
stating that and forward it to the assistant DA on the case.

I had a bowl of soup for dinner, then turned my attention to
Catherine's second bequest. What in the world was I going to do
about her great-grandson? I curled up on the couch and went over
the papers she'd provided one more time.

Danny and Stacy Cooper had married young and quickly produced
two children. According to Catherine's letter, they went kind of crazy
at first—buying all kinds of things for the babies and their first apartment—and ended up with some serious credit problems before their
third anniversary. But they'd been trying to correct all that ever since.

I caught a movement out of the corner of my eye. Curtis, still crawling low, slipped out from behind the plant and slowly made his way
toward the kitchen. I paid him no attention and went back to work.

Danny Cooper hadn't just worked two jobs, he got three and evidently put all he had into getting out of debt. In only a little over two years, he'd worked his way up to a supervisor's spot at the paper company there in Fitzgerald. Stacy was no slouch either, putting in long hours at a daycare center. They'd paid off their overdue bills, kept current on the rest, and even started saving money for a house. Their credit was on the mend.

Normally they'd have had to wait a few more years before buying a house. But then Jim Lazenby entered the picture. Catherine had described him as a real estate man who owned a lot of property in the county.

Stacy and Danny initially wanted to rent one of his houses, but Lazenby offered them a better deal. All they had to do was put $8,000 down on the house, rent it for a year and then buy it. When they explained they didn't have that much money saved, Lazenby offered to let them pay extra every month until they reached $8,000. The money would go into an escrow account for the down payment until it was time for them to purchase the house.

It seemed like the perfect arrangement. Their credit was still recovering, but they believed they'd be able to qualify for a mortgage in another year, especially with a nice down payment waiting in the bank. In the meantime, they'd live in a nice house with a big yard for the children.

They took Lazenby up on his offer, handed over every penny they'd saved as a start on the down payment and moved in. And every month they paid the rent plus more money into escrow. The lease they signed required them to buy the house within one year. The deadline had been the previous February.

But things were tight in February. There were some medical expenses and one of their cars broke down. They'd already managed to pay Lazenby the full down payment amount and could probably have scraped together enough for the closing costs and gotten the mortgage, but it would have been a stretch.

Then Lazenby stepped up and appeared to save the day. He told them it wouldn't matter if they wanted to wait a few months; he didn't mind putting off the sale for a while. Unfortunately, that statement was never reduced to writing—at least I couldn't find anything like that in the papers Catherine had left for me. But the Coopers were relieved that Lazenby was willing to work with them. They thought everything was just fine.

Then in March they were served with an eviction notice, declaring they had defaulted on the contract. They lost the house and, of course, Lazenby kept their down payment money.

Danny and Stacy tried to fight it. They hired a lawyer. It took months to work through the system, but they finally went to court. Unfortunately, there was no proof that Lazenby had agreed to an extension of the contract. Of course, they lost. The Coopers were out, Lazenby kept the house, and walked away with their money. To put it in legal terms, they had been royally screwed.

I blew out a defeated breath and watched Curtis slink back behind his plant. I still didn't see any way to help the Coopers, but I couldn't just write the situation off and pocket the money. At the very least, I owed Catherine the effort of going to Fitzgerald to hear the story straight from the victims.

It was nearly 8:30 when I called Danny Cooper. After introducing myself and expressing sympathy for the death of his great grandmother, I explained that she'd asked me to look into the situation.

"Are you ... uh ... some kind of lawyer or something, ma'am?"

"No. I work as an investigator in a district attorney's office. But I wouldn't be doing this in any official capacity. Catherine just thought I might see something that had been missed."

"Oh." He sounded doubtful and I didn't blame him. "Okay, I guess that'll be all right."

I told him I could drive down the next day.

"If you can be here around noon, I can come home for lunch."

He gave me directions and I told him I'd see him tomorrow.

I heard a scratching noise from the hallway. Evidently Curtis had found and made use of the cat box.

The next couple of hours passed quickly with me staring at the computer screen, seeing what I could find on Jim Lazenby. James Hinton Lazenby, I discovered, was a pretty high profile guy in Fitzgerald, Georgia. JCs, Rotary, Chamber of Commerce. On the surface, he was a regular pillar of the community. There was a story in the local paper about the kids' baseball team his real estate company sponsored and he and his wife Robin were familiar faces on the local society pages. Pictures of the two at country club dances and charity events showed a smiling, well-dressed couple in their forties.

Jim was a tall, good-looking man with dark hair and a salesman's smile. He wasn't fat, but had the soft look of someone who didn't exercise much. His wife, petite, stylish, with lots of blonde hair, smiled as brightly as her husband, but in some of the photos her eyes had a vague, glassed-over stare that hinted at boredom or some sort of chemical involvement.

Delving a little deeper under that glossy surface, I found another story. There'd been several complaints to the Better Business

Bureau about his home sales and his dealings with his tenants. He'd been sued on at least four occasions, but court records never showed any judgments against him. The most interesting thing I picked up was a hint that Lazenby might be getting into politics. The state senate seemed to be his immediate goal and I guessed his name might be on the ballot when the elections rolled around next year.

After the eleven o'clock news, I headed for bed, firmly closing my bedroom door behind me. I didn't really think Curtis would attack me, but the idea of him suddenly leaping up on the bed in the middle of the night was unsettling.

FIVE

IT WAS THE SCREAM THAT WOKE ME — SHRILL AND AGO-
nized. My feet hit the floor before I was even fully awake. I ran
from the room, expecting to find someone or something horribly
injured — and almost tripped over the cat. He was sitting right outside the bedroom door and, as I watched, he raised his head toward the ceiling, opened his mouth and issued another one of those
screams.

"What the *hell* is wrong with you?"

Curtis looked at me once, then scooted around my feet and shot
into the bedroom. I followed, switching on the light. Just what I
needed. First I inherited a cat and now he'd lost his mind.

At least I didn't have to search for him this time. He was sitting
on the foot of my bed. As I walked up to him, he turned in a circle,
lay down and closed his eyes. I guessed that he must have slept on
Catherine's bed and now he was making himself at home on mine.

For a minute, I stood there considering my options. I could
snatch him up and close him out of the room again, but he'd probably just keep screaming. Or I could go back to bed and hope he
didn't try to kill me in my sleep. I went for the second option. It just
seemed easier and, at three in the morning, I was all for easy.

The rest of the night passed peacefully—until I woke around 6:15 to Curtis standing beside my pillow, head-butting my shoulder—cat speak, I gathered, for "feed me".

"You'll have to wait a bit," I told him. "First things first. Besides, I haven't forgiven you yet for last night."

I showered and dressed before giving into his demands. It was important to establish who was in charge here.

I over-filled Curtis's food bowl and left him plenty of water. Then I scooped out the litter box and deposited the waste in the trash. Confident that he'd be fine until I got home that afternoon, I left the house.

Wednesday was chilly, gray and rainy. It was just 7:00 when I climbed into the Trailblazer and hit the button to open the garage door. The weather guesser on the early morning radio news declared the rain would continue until late afternoon and the temperature wouldn't climb out of the 50s. It wasn't the perfect day for a road trip, but I wanted to get this over with.

In my rearview mirror I saw Milton Overton, dressed in a bright yellow slicker, gliding around the cul de sac in his golf cart. It was barely daylight, but here he was, the self-appointed enforcer of all neighborhood covenants on his self-appointed rounds. He stopped in front of a house a few doors down and reached for a notepad. Another poor soul must have run afoul of the HOA rules and Milt was just the guy to document it.

Ignoring Milt the Snitch, as he was not-so-affectionately known, I punched Danny Cooper's address into the GPS app on my phone. Moments later, I left the neighborhood, following the commands of the cheerful, but assertive female voice that indicated when and where I should drive and turn.

Luck was with me that morning. While traffic was heavy and there were the expected slow downs, no major incident stopped the rush hour dead in its tracks. I was on the south side of Atlanta in an hour and a half.

I kept the radio tuned to WSB to try and stay on top of the traffic situation. Every half hour, there was a newscast. One story that was repeated each time was that a "grandmother had been killed in a multi-car accident" the evening before. I figured that even if she'd been a nuclear physicist, this woman would never be called anything else. I'd noticed that any person over a certain age mentioned in a news story was referred to as either a grandparent or an elderly man or woman.

Fitzgerald was a town in Ben Hill County in the extreme southern part of the state. I'd never been there. In fact, I tried not to visit south Georgia at all if I could help it because I hated venturing below the gnat line. Billions of the tiny swarming insects inhabit the southern part of the state. They're so much a part of life that the natives hardly notice them. I once had a conversation with a man outside a restaurant in Valdosta who had two gnats crawling along his eyelid and never even blinked!

The gnat line isn't some crazy legend. It does exist, following the fall line that runs diagonally across the middle of the state, dividing the piedmont from the coastal plain. North of the line is rolling countryside and eventually the Appalachian foothills. South of the line, where an ancient sea once lay, the land levels out. Hills disappear and the gnats thrive, undisturbed by the breezes or altitude of the northern half of Georgia.

Summer is the worst time for the pests. During the winter, most of them left or died or hibernated or something. Now that the weather had grown cool, I hoped the second week of November might be relatively gnat free.

Interstate 75 is one of the most heavily traveled north/south arteries in the country and that day it more than lived up to its reputation. Of the vehicles traveling south with me, over half seemed to be huge semis that crowded side by side in the lanes and left drenching sprays of water in their wakes. I didn't relax my grip on the wheel until traffic thinned out well south of Macon.

The rain finally stopped as I was closing in on Fitzgerald. This was farm country, although most of the year's crops had already been harvested. Along the roadside the gray ghosts of summer weeds and wildflowers still stood upright, swaying stiffly in the light wind. Small houses and barns dotted the landscape. Most of the fall glory around my house had faded and leaves were falling fast, but here in the southern part of the state, the autumn color was just beginning and many of the trees were still green.

With every turn of the tires, my seven-year-old Trailblazer guzzled more gas. I'd already filled up once and would have to do it again soon. The hulking beast had been awarded to me in the divorce settlement and I hated it more every time I pulled up to a gas pump. But it was paid for and hadn't given me any real problems. And today's gas was on Catherine.

When I was still ten miles or so outside of Fitzgerald itself, the GPS began rattling off commands. I obeyed, left the expressway, and turned onto a country road. I passed through a little community called Irwinville and about a mile beyond that, still following the mechanical voice, turned onto Tom Jodson Road. It was a narrow, paved track that wound through heavy pine woods.

After half a mile or so, the GPS directed me onto an even smaller road. I passed a beat-up trailer in an overgrown yard. Around a curve was a second dwelling—a one-story frame structure that had once been white, but was now a weathered gray. It had begun life as a farmhouse maybe 45 or 50 years before. Now it was a ramshackle rental on the edge of someone else's pasture. The mechanical voice announced I'd reached my destination.

I got out of the car cautiously, tensed and ready for an onslaught of gnats, but there was no sign of the nasty things. I permitted myself a relieved sigh, enjoying the gentle wind from the northwest that brushed my face. It was warmer here than at home, but there was still a touch of autumn in the air.

The front door opened and a young woman stepped out on the sagging porch. She was a big girl—5'10" or more and easily 150 pounds. But she wasn't fat, just tall and shapely and very pretty. Shiny brown hair fell nearly to her waist and her lightly freckled face glowed with health and good cheer. Two small blonde heads, one about four inches above the other, appeared around the door jamb.

"Miz Christopher?"

I smiled. "Yes. Please call me Emily. You must be Stacy."

"Yes, ma'am. And these two wild savages are Brittany and Micah."

The children giggled. We shook hands and I followed her into the house, the children leading the way. The walls hadn't seen fresh paint in a couple of decades and the floors were worn, scuffed and sloping. The house was furnished with what were probably hand-me-downs, but happy family photos hung on the walls and there was a comfortable, inviting air about the place.

Down a short hallway was the kitchen where the table was set for three.

"I hope you're hungry," Stacy said. "Danny'll be home any minute now and he's always starving."

We spent the next few minutes chatting about the weather and the upcoming holidays. I tried to talk a bit with the little girl, but at three years old, Brittany had a limited vocabulary and a definite suspicion of strangers. Micah was about a year younger and babbled, but not in any language I could understand.

It was a relief for all of us when the sound of a rattling engine from the yard signaled that Danny was home. He gave his wife and children kisses, then he held his hand out to me, smiling politely.

"Pleased to meet you, ma'am." His hand was rough, but clean. His blue pants and uniform shirt were neatly pressed, but a little big for his thin frame. "I surely appreciate you coming all this way to talk to us. I didn't know Grandma Catherine would do something like this."

"She was worried about you."

"Seems like. But I can't see there's anything you can do about this mess."

Stacy wasn't ready for that discussion yet. "Let's have something to eat before we get all serious."

She directed us to the table. "The kids already had their lunch." She put a platter of sandwiches—bologna and cheese on white bread—on the table, along with a plate of sliced tomatoes and a bag of potato chips.

"Now y'all be sure and eat plenty of tomatoes. Those are the last we're going to get this year. I picked 'em green and let 'em ripen on the window sill."

The food took me back to the comforting lunches of my childhood. I ate every bite of my sandwich, several slices of tomato, and accepted a refill on the sweet tea. When we were done, Stacy cleared away the dishes and Danny fetched a good-sized cardboard box from the hall closet. He pulled out a stack of papers and laid them on the table. Then, while his children played on the floor around the table, he explained what had happened.

The contract, a rent-to-own agreement for a house on Bayberry Court, was only three pages long.

"That's it," Danny said. "That's what he used to steal our money."

I gave it a quick once over. Although I hadn't seen a copy of the actual document before, it was just as Catherine had described it. "How much were you paying a month?"

"Like it says there—$650."

"But we paid more," Stacy said. "Every single month we gave him an extra $350 to go to the down payment. He said that if he kept it instead of us we'd be less tempted to spend it. That's the money he stole."

"How much was the down payment?"

"$8,000. We paid extra every month until he had it all."

"Yeah," Danny said. "Then we got those papers saying we were going to be evicted."

"Did you miss any rent payments?"

"No, ma'am. Not a single one. A few times me and Stacy went to work when we were sick to be sure we had the money to make those payments."

"Were you ever late with a payment?"

"Never once."

"We had to go without some stuff to have the money for Mr. Lazenby," Stacy said. "Just us, now," she added hurriedly, "not the kids. But we always had that money when he come to the door on the first of the month."

"Came to the door? You mean Lazenby personally collected the rent money at your house?" That sounded like something from another century.

Stacy nodded. "He knew I got home from work by 4:00 every day and he was always there by 5:00 on the first of the month with his hand out."

"That's right," Danny said. "And he always wanted cash—not a money order or anything else. Just cash. He came every month. He goes to all his houses on the first of the month to pick up the rent, starts early in the morning and makes a day of it. Everybody knows it. Once he gets the money, he puts it in an old briefcase in the trunk of his car. Don't know where it goes from there." Danny's blue eyes narrowed. "People say he does it that way so he doesn't have to pay taxes on it."

"How many rental houses does this guy own?" I asked.

"Twenty or thirty, maybe."

"Did you get a receipt when you paid the rent?" I asked.

"Sure did." Stacy pointed to the stack of papers. "They're all in there. We kept every single one so no one could say we missed a payment. We wanted to do everything just right."

Danny suddenly stood up as if he couldn't contain the anger building within him and had to let some of it out in a burst of activity. "He just stole it from us and I let him! I shoulda been smarter. I shoulda known what he was doing. I'm just so stupid!"

He brought the side of his fist down on the old kitchen counter, rattling dishes and startling the children.

Stacy went to him and put her arms around him. "Honey, you

didn't know. Nobody would have. Mr. Lazenby's the one to blame here, not you. Now come back and sit down and let's see what Miss Emily can do to help us."

He followed his wife back to the table and dropped into his chair, his hands clenched on the table top. I could see him forcing himself to relax. "Sorry. It just makes me so mad sometimes …"

"So tell me what happened."

"Ten A."

"What?"

"Ten A is what happened." He flipped to the second page of the contract, pushed it over to me and tapped the middle of the paper with a forefinger. "Right there. That's what got us."

Paragraph 10-A was short, but deadly. It set out the terms for the purchase of the house. When Stacy and Danny signed the contract, they agreed to purchase the house by February 21 of this year. That meant they had to make the down payment, have financing arranged, and close the sale by that date. Failure to do so would result in their losing the house and forfeiting any down payment money — referred to as earnest money — Lazenby held.

"So you didn't close by the date in the contract?"

Danny looked down at his hands. "No, ma'am. We should have, I know. And everything would have been okay. But Brittany got a bad ear infection and had to have some special medicine and then the car broke down…" He expelled a frustrated breath. "Oh, it don't matter why. We just didn't have the money for the closing."

"But we talked to Mr. Lazenby about it," Stacy said. "And he told us not to worry, that he'd just extend the contract for another year. We thought everything was fine until those papers came in March."

I was sure I knew the answer, but I asked the question anyway. "Did you get that extension in writing?"

The young couple exchanged an embarrassed look. "No," Danny said. "We just shook hands on it. Later he claimed he never said that."

"Was anyone else there when he told you that?"

Stacy just shook her head.

"No," Danny said. "There weren't any witnesses, if that's what you're asking."

They'd done what they could to salvage the situation. When talking to Lazenby didn't help, they hired a lawyer and fought the eviction in court. But they lost, of course. The contract was clear. And then they were stuck with $1,500 worth of attorney's fees on top of everything else.

"We found out later this wasn't the only time Mr. Lazenby's got away with somebody's down payment money. He's done it a lot before."

Stacy agreed. "Only problem is that he always manages to keep it legal."

SIX

I ASKED WHAT THEY COULD TELL ME ABOUT LAZENBY HIM-self. Their information just underlined what I'd found online. The man was a local success story. He'd grown up in Fitzgerald, the son of working class parents. He'd never shown great aptitude in school, but he had one real talent. He could run like a rabbit while carrying a football. In a small town, that'll get you a long way.

"There's still a picture of him in the school lobby," Danny said. "In a case with the state championship trophy they won back in 1987."

Lazenby had been captain of his high school football team and then gone on to play for the University of Georgia. But things didn't turn out quite like he expected there. He discovered that, at the college level, there were a lot of young men who could run with the football.

"He did okay," Danny said. "You know, played some for the Bulldogs and even went to a bowl game, but he wasn't ever a real star. And he just wasn't good enough for the NFL."

So Lazenby had hooked his wagon to another star — this one from his own hometown. Robin Walker was the only child of older, wealthy parents. She and Lazenby had dated through high school and she, too, attended the University. They'd married right after their senior year.

No one was surprised that Lazenby joined Robin's dad's real estate firm. Now twenty-something years later, the elder Walker had conveniently died and Jim owned the whole thing, along with the string of rental houses the Coopers had mentioned.

The Lazenbys had two children—a daughter still in high school and a son in his sophomore year at FSU.

"So what kind of person is he?" I asked.

Danny and Stacy spoke simultaneously.

"Smooth," she said.

"Mean," was her husband's contribution. He glanced at her and shrugged. "Yeah, I guess you could say he's smooth, too. He can be real charming when he wants to. That's the face he wears at his office and the country club and places like that. But he's got a mean streak a mile wide. He's put a bunch of folks out on the street, just like us, and it doesn't bother him a bit."

"And maybe he's done more than that," Stacy added.

Danny frowned. "Now we don't know that, babe. You're just repeating gossip."

"I'd like to hear the gossip," I said.

He took a deep breath. "Few years back, Lazenby and another guy in town, Franklin Eckley got together to build this new subdivision on the north side of town, out like you're going to Queensland. It was going to be the fanciest place in Fitzgerald to live. Except they ran out of money before they could get any houses built. This was back when the recession was really getting started.

"Folks said they were both going to go bankrupt, but then Franklin ... died. It was a car crash out on Ten Mile Road. It's a real straight stretch of highway. The police said he must have swerved to miss a deer, ran off the road and hit a tree."

"It happens," I said.

"Maybe, but it was sure a lucky deer for Jim Lazenby." Danny began replacing the papers in the box. "Since they were partners, they each had life insurance to pay the other one if something happened to either of 'em. Business insurance, I guess it was. Anyhow, Franklin's insurance paid off all the money they owed on that subdivision, so Jim got out of the jam without a scratch."

"Did he finish building the place?"

"Naw. Way the economy's been, nobody's building anything. All that's there is this big fine road and a lot of weeds. But with things looking up, it might still happen."

"What about his wife, is it Robin?"

Stacy rolled her eyes. "Now Robin's a whole different story. I heard she was always kinda flaky. Loves the social scene—parties, country club—and she likes her martinis. From what some of the ladies in town say, she can drink grown men right under the table. Oh, and a couple of years ago she opened this little shop.

"Everyone thought it'd be a gift shop or something, you know, the kind of thing rich ladies do when their kids grow up and they're bored. But ..." She burst out laughing.

"What did she do? Open a sex shop or something?"

"No, it's not that bad. But it is crazy. She calls it Chakra and she sells all this magic stuff. You know, fortune telling cards and charms and crystals. Me and my friend Kendra went in there one day." She laughed again. "It was really weird! She has this big ol' bin full of polished rocks and she'll sell you a little leather bag full of them for $30. For a bag of rocks!"

Stacy laughed some more, but Danny just shook his head. "I think she's just a sad lady looking for something to help her. Life with Jim Lazenby can't be a whole lot of fun. Everybody knows he runs around on her. He doesn't even try to hide it."

At the end of an hour, Danny and Stacy had told me everything they knew about the Lazenbys. They'd made copies of all their paperwork and gave them to me as we walked out to my car.

"We really appreciate you coming all the way down here," Danny told me. "It means a lot that you're willing to help."

I shook his hand, but cautioned, "I don't know if I'll be able to do anything for you. I honestly don't see any way to get the money back."

He nodded. "I know. But we still thank you for trying."

Before I climbed back into the car, I asked them to do me a favor. "Don't tell anyone about me coming down, okay? I'll have a better chance of helping you if no one knows."

"Yes, ma'am," Stacy said. "You can count on us to keep quiet."

They stood side by side in the drive, waving as I drove away.

This trip had probably been a waste of my time and theirs. I felt bad for raising their hopes even a little. Lazenby was a low life who cheated people for a living, but from what I could tell, it looked like he kept it just legal enough to get by. I could have just ended it right then and told myself I'd done everything I could, but I kept remembering Catherine bringing me that damned soup.

It was nearly one and, if I left any later, I'd be stuck in the stranglehold of Atlanta's afternoon rush hour, but I hated to come all this way with nothing to show for it. When I got to the highway at the end of Tom Jodson Road, instead of turning right to go back to the interstate, I turned left toward town. Maybe I'd be able to turn up something in Fitzgerald. If I started back by 4:00, I'd still be home at a decent hour and miss the traffic.

SEVEN

FITZGERALD IS THE COUNTY SEAT OF BEN HILL COUNTY
and was a something of a surprise. I'd expected the usual small
country town, but the downtown section was crisscrossed by
wide, multi-laned boulevards with grassy, well-kept medians. Live
oak trees lined the streets in the historic section where gracious
old homes were lovingly cared for. I drove around a bit, hoping
to get a sense of the place and trying to decide what my first stop
should be. I could do some more research — I've always believed
you can't have too much information — or go straight to Lazenby's
office and try to make him see reason and political reality.

A tiny, brightly-colored rooster strolled nonchalantly across the
street and I slammed on the brakes to avoid hitting it. What was it
doing here? As I watched, the little bird hopped over a curb onto
an immaculate lawn where he joined two other exotically-hued
birds, pecking the grass for insect snacks. Minutes later I saw more
of the small birds congregated in the side yard of a big red brick
house.

I had no logical explanation for the city livestock, so I put the
chickens out of my mind and got to work. From what I'd learned
so far, Lazenby was a ruthless, greedy man, but he worked hard to

maintain his glossy social facade. He was active in service organizations and firmly grounded in the local social life.

He was a sleaze, but a sleaze with political ambitions. Maybe I could talk him into refunding some of the Coopers' money, just to be nice—and to avoid any kind of public embarrassment right when he was trying hard to appear squeaky clean.

According to my notes, Lazenby Realty was located on East Pine Street. I put the address in the GPS and, two minutes later, was parking the Trailblazer in the lot beside the single-story brick building. Concrete containers of bright chrysanthemums flanked the entrance.

The waiting area was furnished with molded plastic chairs and current magazines and, at the receptionist's desk, a woman who was guaranteed to make a favorable impression on customers. The name plate on her desk identified her as Cheryl Pressley. She was probably in her late 20s. Her hair was a mass of curls and her luminous skin was the color of coffee with cream. When she smiled, it lit up the whole room.

"May I help you?"

"Yes. I wondered if Mr. Lazenby could see me."

She asked for my name and I gave it. "Let me just check." She picked up her phone, punched two numbers and spoke quietly. Then she gave me another big smile. "He'll be right with you, Ms. Christopher."

As I was thanking her, the man himself emerged from an office down the hall.

"Hello, there." Lazenby stuck out his hand and I had no choice but to shake it. "Jim Lazenby."

"Emily Christopher," I said. I released the grip as quickly as I could. "Nice to meet you."

"What can we do for you, Miz Christopher? Looking for a house?"

"Could I talk with you — in private?"

He shrugged. "Sure."

He led me down the hall into a large office. The walls were covered with framed awards and certificates and photos of Lazenby with a variety of people. I'd never seen most of them, but I did recognize the governor and a former senator.

Lazenby sat behind a desk that was big and cluttered and gestured at the two chairs in front of him. I took the one closest to the door.

"I wanted to talk to you about a young couple. Danny and Stacy Cooper. They . . . rented a house from you last year, but then they were evicted."

"Yes, I was sorry I had to do that." His face took on a sad, sanctimonious expression. "In this economy, we've seen way too many people lose their houses. I sure hope they get back on their feet soon."

"That's where I was hoping you could help."

"Excuse me, but just how are you involved in this?"

"I'm just trying to help Stacy and Danny. I guess you'd say I'm a friend of the family." I kept my answer as vague as I could. "But about the Coopers — they've had a rough time. They lost the house and their down payment. They both work hard and they've got two little kids. If they could just get that money back — even part of it — it would go a long way in putting them back on the right road."

He frowned a bit. "Surely you're not suggesting that I reward those two deadbeats by giving them money, are you? It's not my fault they lost the house."

Behind his head was a certificate proclaiming Lazenby 2014 Businessman of the Year. I tried to keep my voice pleasant. "I know they didn't abide by the contract, Mr. Lazenby, and they weren't able to buy the house by the designated date, but I think they might have misunderstood something you said to them about… "

"Something I *said*?"

"They believed that you extended the contract when they told you they were having financial problems."

"That's ridiculous! I'm a businessman, not a social worker. And are you an attorney, Miz Christopher?"

"No, I'm not."

"Then perhaps you don't fully understand that a contract is a contract." The smile was long gone, replaced by a sneer.

"I do understand that, Mr. Lazenby. But I'm hoping you're willing to give the Coopers some credit for what they did right. They were faithful in paying the rent every month on time. And they were able to give you the whole down payment within that year. They were trying so hard."

"The truth is they didn't hold up their side of the bargain. They didn't buy that house by the deadline." A mean note crept into his voice. "They might have been *trying* hard, as you say, but those kind of people never seem to get it right, do they? Buying shit they can't afford, popping out brats every other year and expecting the rest of us to take care of them. Good intentions don't mean a goddamn thing where the law is concerned. They got exactly what they deserved."

How had this man lived so long without somebody shooting him? It was clear I couldn't appeal to his better nature; he didn't have one. A change in tactics was called for.

47

I took a deep breath. "No, I guess they don't. But good intentions might mean something to the voters."

"What the hell is that supposed to mean?"

"Just that a story in the local paper about how you took pity on a poor young couple down on their luck might go a long way in helping in your run for the legislature. It sure would read better than a piece about poor people losing their down payments in your rent-to-buy deals. I know the Coopers weren't the first. Probably not the last either. It wouldn't be hard to find the whole list…"

He stood up, shoved a pile of papers to one side and leaned across his desk at me, eyes narrowed in fury. "What do you know about me? Do you think you can just waltz in here and threaten me? I don't take shit from anybody, lady. Not you or anybody! People who take me on sometimes lose more than they expect."

"I only…"

He got to his feet, pushing back his chair so fast it nearly tipped over. "Get the hell out of here! Right now, before I call the sheriff and have your ass arrested for trespassing!"

I left the office as quickly as I could with Lazenby right behind me, up the hall and past the receptionist whose eyes had widened with alarm. He stood on the sidewalk in front of his office and watched as I got back in my car and drove out of the parking lot.

The deep breath I took as I turned the corner was a little shaky. I wasn't surprised that pleading the Coopers' case to Lazenby hadn't helped. I'd expected him to refuse, but I hadn't anticipated that degree of anger. I don't like being yelled at any more than the next person, but it's happened before and never really bothered me.

However, the encounter with Lazenby was different. There was something about the man that hinted of darkness and violence just beneath the surface. It was hard to put into words, but I felt like I'd spent time with something cold-blooded and not quite human.

There really wasn't anything else for me to do in Fitzgerald. The Coopers weren't going to get their money back and I felt like I'd just wasted a day. A glance at my watch showed it was only 2:05. So I decided to kill some time rounding out the research on Jim Lazenby.

At the library on Main Street a soft-spoken young woman named Lakeesha pointed me to a row of computers against a back wall.

"We've got the newspapers back to 2005 online. Before that, it's all microfilm," she told me. "We're trying to catch up, but it takes forever and it's real boring work!"

She showed me the indexes and made sure I understood how to operate the machines before leaving me alone.

"Oh, one more thing," I asked before she got away. "What's the story with those chickens I've been seeing around town?"

She turned back to me, a grin on her face. "Oh, the chickens! Aren't they something? They're all over the place. People either hate 'em or love 'em. I kinda love 'em myself. 'Course I don't live right here in town where they wake me up crowing every morning."

"But why are they here? In town, I mean."

"That's a good story," she said, leaning her back against a big gray microfilm cabinet. "The DNR did it. You know, the Department of Natural Resources. They were trying to introduce another game bird to the state, like quail or something. So they got these Burmese chickens and took 'em out in the woods around the state and let 'em go. They were supposed to get established and live out in the wild and then folks could go hunt 'em. But most of the colonies were failures. They didn't reproduce and just died out."

She grinned again. "Except for here. In Ben Hill County, the chickens did okay. But they didn't like the woods and they came to town instead. Now they're all over the place. They're pretty little things. Some people put out seed for them and think of 'em as pets. Other folks spend their time running 'em out of their yards. They do make a mess."

She shook her head. "But you can't kill 'em. It's against the law. In fact, the town has a festival for 'em every spring. The Wild Chicken Festival."

"What do they do?"

"At the festival? Oh, it's like every other one you see. Food and music and kids' stuff—you know, the usual. Oh, yeah, they also have this chicken crowing contest." She laughed. "Now that can be something to watch."

She left me to my work, but stopped by several times to see if I needed anything. I'd already seen most everything they had online about Lazenby, so I checked stories on Franklin Eckley's death. It was pretty much what the Coopers had told me. In late December of 2009, there was a small story on page three about the single-car accident in which Eckley was killed. A day later the paper carried his obituary. A well-liked businessman, he'd been 38 at the time of his death, unmarried and a member of the First Baptist Church. There was no mention of any association with Jim Lazenby.

Next came microfilm. I checked the index for Lazenby and pulled several reels of the film. I didn't find anything of interest after forty-five uncomfortable minutes in the hard metal chair staring at the flickering screen. By 3:00, I was finished.

The county courthouse was only a few blocks away, so I left my car in the library lot and walked. In the Clerk of Court's Office an efficient woman about my own age helped get me started looking up deeds. The process was a weird mixture of archaic and modern. I started with huge, leather-bound registers, turning two-foot wide pages to find the entries I needed, then moments later, followed the trail into cyberspace. Once I got the hang of it, it was easy and it took less than an hour to discover that Jim Lazenby owned 34 houses in Ben Hill County. Over half of them had belonged to Robin's father. Lazenby also owned, either wholly or partly, four businesses and three large tracts of land outside the city.

In another section of the Clerk's Office, I found Lazenby had been named in seven separate lawsuits, all related to real estate in one way or another, but there'd never been a judgment against him.

Not knowing if I'd ever need them, I paid over $170 of Catherine's money for copies of all those deeds and lawsuits. I carried the stack of copies back to the library parking lot and climbed in the car.

It was past 4:00 and driving back through Atlanta would be no problem now. But since I was already here, I decided to take a quick look at the property at the heart of the Coopers' situation. The GPS made it as easy as entering an address.

EIGHT

THE RAIN WAS BACK, ALTHOUGH IT WAS MORE A DRIZZLE than a downpour. East Central Avenue changed to Jacksonville Highway when I left the city limits and the surroundings grew more rural. A few miles out, I located a small subdivision on the left. The frame houses were of varying shades of brown and beige. Two turns brought me to Bayberry Court.

I knew that driving out here to see the house the Coopers had lost was pointless. It had already changed hands and there was nothing here that would help get back their money. But for some reason it seemed important to see what had been taken from them.

I stopped in front of what had been Stacy and Danny Cooper's dream of home ownership. It was a split-foyer model, nearly indistinguishable from its neighbors. A green Toyota was parked in the drive and a pink tricycle lay on its side near the front door. It made me sad to think of what the Coopers almost had.

My watch read quarter to five. Time to head home. As I left the subdivision and turned toward town, an old gray pickup, which had been parked on the side of the highway, pulled back onto the pavement and fell in close behind me. I got the Trailblazer up to speed, but the truck didn't back off. He not only matched my speed, he actually seemed to be getting closer.

"Jackass," I muttered. I hate people who tailgate. There was no oncoming traffic. "Go around me."

I even slowed down to make his passing easier, but he stayed right where he was and I felt the first stirring of uneasiness. I sped up. So did the pickup. Its tinted windows kept me from seeing the driver, but his intentions soon became clear. He got even closer and nudged my back bumper. At 60 miles an hour, a nudge is a terrible thing. The wheel jerked in my hand and I had to fight to stay on the road.

The highway ahead was straight and empty, flanked on both sides by pine woods and pastures. There were no houses or businesses along this stretch where I could go for help. And I was afraid to take my hands off the wheel long enough to find my phone and dial 911. My only hope was to outrun him. I pushed down the accelerator and the speedometer climbed to 70, then 75. The truck stayed right with me.

When he pulled up beside me on the left, I knew what he was going to do, but was powerless to stop him. I could, however, lower the speed of the impact. I hit the brakes hard so I'd have more control when he pulled into the side of my car.

The impact was loud, metal against protesting metal. The back end of the SUV suddenly had a life of its own, fishtailing, then drifting toward the shoulder. The rest of the car followed in an erratic counterclockwise manner.

Then I was bumping over rough terrain, through trees and underbrush, dropping backward away from the highway. The brakes and the steering wheel did nothing to slow or guide the car. In the end, all I could do was hold on and wonder if this would be where I died, on a country road on a rainy November day.

The car came to an abrupt stop with the front right wheel in a gully. The seatbelt caught me as I was thrown forward at the same time the airbag smacked me in the face. And then everything was still.

With a trembling hand, I fought down the deflating airbag and switched off the ignition. I unfastened the belt and climbed out on shaking legs that barely held me upright, checking myself for injuries. Except for a bruised lip and a sore shoulder where I'd bounced off the door, I seemed to be all right. I'd started around the SUV to get some idea of the damages when I heard a squeal of tires and looked up through the trees at the highway.

The pickup was back. A door opened, then slammed. A moment later, a man walked around the truck and looked down the slight incline to where I stood beside my car. All I could tell from that distance was that he was big, white, with longish hair, and was apparently disappointed he hadn't done the job. He grabbed a baseball bat out of the cab and started running in my direction.

I hesitated for half a second. My first instinct was to make a stand, but I didn't have any kind of weapon and was certainly no physical match for this guy. So I ran — as fast as I could into the thick woods behind me.

There was no path — just trees and heavy undergrowth. Wet branches slapped my face and arms, and briars tore at skin and clothes, but I never slowed. It wasn't long until I heard him crashing through the woods behind me.

The knee I'd twisted playing tennis last month began sending frantic signals to my brain in the form of serious pain, but I couldn't

stop. I ran a crazy, zigzag route until I came to an area completely covered by kudzu. Shoving back some of the vines, I made an
opening large enough to climb through. The interior was dark and
damp. I slipped inside, then pulled the vines back across the hole
and focused on slowing my breathing.

Seconds later I heard him, blundering through the underbrush,
out of breath and cursing. I concentrated on being absolutely still
and silent. He didn't slow his pace at my hiding place, just pushed
on through the woods. I relaxed, but only a little. When he didn't
find me up ahead, I knew he'd come back this way.

The luminous dial on my watch showed it was twenty minutes
after 5:00. It would be dark in less than an hour, probably sooner
with the cloud cover. I carefully shifted an inch or two, trying to
get comfortable on the soggy ground. My knee throbbed and my
clothes stuck to my skin. The temperature had dropped to the point
where it was chilly and a shiver went through me. I hoped I hadn't
stumbled into a rattlesnake's winter home.

It seemed to take forever, but was actually only about fifteen
minutes before my attacker returned. His progress was slower this
time, but he didn't stop anywhere near me. Here under the dense
pines, it had grown so dark that I doubted he'd see me if I were
standing out in the open.

Still he continued to thrash around and now he was shouting.
"Where are you, bitch? When I find you, you're really going to be
sorry!" There was a strangled cry and a muffled crash. He must have
fallen. "*Where are you?*" His voice broke with fury.

After a few more minutes, the sounds of his cursing and lum-
bering through the dark woods grew fainter. Finally, there came a
time when I couldn't hear him any longer. I hoped he was gone, but

wasn't ready to move just yet. Another ten minutes passed before I cautiously climbed out of my leafy cave, straining my eyes to find him in the darkness.

As far as I could tell, I was alone. Now what? I'll be the first to admit I'm not a woodsman — or woodswoman — especially at night, in the rain, shaking with cold. Even if I could have found my way back to the car, and there was no guarantee I could retrace my erratic path, it probably wasn't a good idea. The man with the bat was no doubt waiting for me to come back to my vehicle. That's what I'd do in his place.

So, I wondered, looking around, where did I go from here? There were no lights visible and no sound reached my ears except the whisper of the misty rain.

Knowing I had to start moving, I set out in the direction roughly opposite from where I'd come. The rain increased to a moderate drizzle. My knee, now swollen and really painful, slowed me some, but that wasn't necessarily a bad thing. The careful pace probably saved me from falling in the rough terrain.

Darkness was complete by 6:30 and panic was beginning to tighten my chest. I was shivering. Dressed only in jeans, a T shirt and a pullover sweater, all of which were now soaking wet, I knew I'd never stay warm through the coming night.

How cold did it get in south Georgia in November? What were the first symptoms of hypothermia? Just to make myself a bit more miserable, I kept remembering news stories about people being lost for days or weeks in the wilderness, some not making it out alive. In my case, I was sure the headline would read "Grandmother Dies of Exposure."

I'd heard of people covering themselves with piles of leaves to stay warm, but the thought of digging into the wet, decaying pine needle ground cover was so unpleasant that I couldn't even consider it.

The first time I saw the light—a brief glimpse out of the corner of my eye—I wasn't sure it was real. When I looked more closely, foliage blocked any view I might have had. But after a few steps, there it was again, twinkling beyond the restless pine branches. I cautiously started in that direction, afraid to take my eyes off the tiny beacon, afraid it would disappear again. But it stayed right there and grew brighter as I got nearer.

NINE

IT WAS A SMALL WOODEN HOUSE AND LOOKED A LITTLE RUN-down from the rear, but it must have been someone's home since there was a glow behind one of the windows. I worked my way around the left side. There was heavy vegetation here, too, but this was cultivated. As I brushed against a waist-high bush, the familiar fragrance of rosemary filled the damp evening air.

Light poured from two front windows and lit the porch. Before I reached the steps, the door was opened by a small woman in a long, gray dress. She must have been well over 80. Her white hair was long and straight, hanging over her shoulders and down her back.

"What in the world happened to you?" she asked, peering out into the darkness. "Come in! Come in, you poor thing!"

I hobbled up the steps to her, dodging a small cloth bag that was suspended from the ceiling. She put an arm around me and shepherded me into the house. The room we entered was blessedly warm. The walls were covered with faded paper that must have been put up in the middle of the last century, but the furnishings looked comfortable and the logs burning away in the small fireplace gave the room a cozy feel.

"Oh, you're soaked to the skin! We've got to fix that right now."

At her direction, I went down the hall into a small bathroom. She brought me a terry cloth robe and a pair of thick socks to put on.

"When you're ready, come out and get warm by the fire."

I stripped off the wet clothes, hung them over the shower curtain rod and dried off with a large bath towel. The mirror showed that my face was covered in scratches, but none of them seemed deep or serious. My shivering had just about stopped. By the time I joined her back in the living room, the woman had pulled a rocking chair up near the hearth. I sat and she wrapped a wool throw around my legs.

"There now," she said. She smiled. Pale blue eyes were set in a kind, wrinkled face. "You're going to feel better in no time."

She bustled into the kitchen while I gave the room a closer look. There were a couple of easy chairs and a long wooden table against the far wall. And then there were the frogs—porcelain, wooden, metal, too many to count—crowding every shelf of a large bookcase.

A few minutes later she was back, putting a hot cup of tea in my hands. I sipped it and felt the warmth flow down my throat.

"That's good. What is it?"

"Chamomile and mint with a little honey. It'll warm you."

I luxuriated in being safe and comfortable. A big black cat dozing on the hearth made me think about Curtis, alone at home, but I'd left him plenty of water and enough dry food for several days. He might not like being left on his own for so long, but he wouldn't be hungry.

"What's your name, honey?"

"Emily Christopher."

She smiled. "Nice to meet you. I'm Imogene Crump. But folks usually call me Miss Gene."

"Thank you so much for helping me," I told her.

She waved my thanks away. "You needed help and I was here. That's usually the way it works." She frowned. "You're scratched up some and, way you were walking, looks like you're hurt."

I nodded and pulled back the throw to have a look at my knee. "I hurt it a few weeks ago. It was getting better, but that run through the woods didn't do it any good."

"I'm sure you'll tell me why you were running through the woods, but first let's see what we can do about your injuries."

A minute later she'd found a wash cloth and antibiotic cream for the cuts on my face and neck. Then she handed me an Ace bandage.

"You want me to do it or you?"

"I'll do it." As I wound the bandage around my knee, I told her about being run off the road and the man who'd chased me through the woods. "I hid in some kudzu until he finally left, but I was afraid to go back to my car."

"Probably good that you didn't." She moved a small ottoman over so that I could put my leg up. When she'd placed an ice pack on my knee and I was covered up again, she asked, "Why was that man chasing you?"

I could have said I didn't know. But for some reason, I found myself pouring out the whole story of Jim Lazenby, the Coopers, and my snooping around town that day.

"All I can figure is that Lazenby didn't like me getting into his business and sent someone out to scare me off—or worse."

Her frown deepened. "Oh, honey, you're lucky you ain't dead.

You couldn't have found a worse one to get mixed up with. That man is pure evil."

Before I could ask anything about Lazenby, she disappeared into the kitchen again. I could hear her opening doors and moving pans. I leaned back in the chair, feeling safe and warm. When I woke, Miss Gene was back, carrying a steaming bowl. She rearranged the ottoman, pulled a small table over in front of me and set the bowl down. One more trip to the kitchen produced two biscuits, a spoon, and a napkin.

"It's vegetable soup. Thought you might be hungry."

Hungry? I realized I was starving. It was all I could do to use the spoon and not gulp it straight from the bowl. I was sorry when I'd finished, because I knew the time had come to get up and get moving.

"That was delicious." I told her. "Now if you wouldn't mind, I'd like to use your phone. I need to call the police and make a report and then get my car pulled out of the ditch and to a garage."

She chuckled. "No garage open this time of night, at least not one that will fix your car. And I can't think that the police could do you much good right now. Fella that wrecked you is long gone. You'd do better to wait 'til morning. You can stay here. Won't be any trouble to me."

"But I couldn't …"

"Sure you could. By then your clothes'll be dry and you'll feel more like doing everything that needs to be done."

It was a relief to agree. I leaned back in the chair, free from having to do anything more tonight.

"Besides," Miss Gene said with a twinkle in those blue eyes, "if you left now you wouldn't hear all about Jim Lazenby—and I got a feeling that's what you need."

"Yes, ma'am," I told her with a smile. "I think that's exactly what I need."

She poured us both another cup of tea and settled back in the easy chair. "I know a lot about what's going on around here, being a witch and all."

TEN

HAD I FALLEN ASLEEP AGAIN? NO, I WAS AWAKE AND IMOGENE
Crump, kindly little old lady, was sitting right there, telling me she
was a witch. It made me a bit uneasy. A person who thought she was
a witch might do anything.

"I . . . I don't understand what . . . "

She laughed delightedly. "Oh, honey, you should see your face!
Wish I had me a camera right now. You look like you expect me
to pull out a broomstick and take a spin around the room!" She
laughed some more.

"Well . . . you said you were a witch."

"Yes, but not the fairy tale kind. And you're not going to find
any books here on wicca or whatever they call that nonsense — nor
devil worship either. I'm a good Christian. But I do what I can to
help folks sometimes — with herbs and things, mostly with advice.
Most people are only looking for somebody to talk to. Usually I just
point out the obvious and give 'em a good dose of common sense."

There in the cozy cabin, she told me her story.

"My sweet husband died back in 1996. He was only 64 years
old." Her eyes focused on something beyond the room. "Bill. I was
lucky to have had him for the thirty years I did. We had our re-

tirement all planned out. We were going to go to Florida—one of those senior communities you hear about—and relax in the sun." She gave a sad sigh. "But we never got there. Things don't always work out like we hope.

"For a while, I thought I'd die, too. Wanted to. But I didn't, of course. The Lord must have wanted me to go on alone. So I did. We never did have children, me and Bill. Might have been easier if we had. After he was gone, I kinda lost interest in all those things that had seemed important before—work and church and making money. We lived in Augusta our whole married life, but I couldn't seem to stay there without him.

"So I went ahead and retired, earlier than I'd planned. Didn't go to Florida though. What do I know about Florida? Bill's old aunt owned this place. She passed on back in the 70s and he inherited it. What were we going to do with an old house and ten acres in the piney woods? Still we held onto it. After all, it was family land and there's an old Crump graveyard in the back. But we hardly ever even came down here."

She got up, put another log on the fire and shifted the wood with a poker until the arrangement suited her and the flames licked around the logs. "You want some more tea?"

"No, thanks. Please, go on with your story."

She sat down again. The cat stirred, stretched, and looked around. It gave me a dismissive look, then went to curl up in Miss Gene's lap.

"Well, I got to thinking about this place. Liked the idea that it was out in the country—didn't have any use for people right then. So I sold the house up in Augusta and moved in on the first day of March in 1997. Been here ever since."

"But how did you get to be a witch? I mean, were you one in Augusta?"

"Lord, no. I was an insurance agent. Never thought about being a witch and I didn't mean to be one here either. It wouldn't have happened at all if it hadn't been for those buzzards and some young hoodlums around here."

Okay, I thought, maybe she *was* crazy. That didn't make any sense at all, but I was too warm and comfortable to care.

"Fitzgerald's got its share of young thugs, like most places," she told me. "Most of 'em don't really mean any harm, just too much energy and not enough to do. 'bout the time I moved here though we were having a lot of vandalism. Mailboxes knocked down, eggs thrown on cars, yard ornaments turned over. And me living 'way out here on my own, I figured I was gonna get a visit from those hellions sooner or later. I thought about buying a gun, but then the buzzards came."

"Buzzards?"

She laughed out loud. "Yep, that was something to see. One morning in April, just as the sun was coming up, I heard all this noise outside. Sounded like some kind of gathering going on, like a big crowd of folks talking low and moving around. Never heard anything like it before." She shook her head at the memory. "I went outside and there was turkey buzzards — those big, ugly birds — all over the yard. They were in the trees, all over the ground, on the roof. There were even some on the porch 'til I shooed 'em off with a broom. A couple of hours later they started to fly off, a few at a time. They were all gone before noon and I thought it was just a one-time thing." She sipped her tea. "But around sunset, they all came back, even more than there'd been that morning. The same thing happened day after day."

I'd never heard of anything like that and didn't care much for the picture her words painted in my mind. "What did you do?"

"Well, I figured there must be some reason for it. You know, birds and other wild animals only do what is natural to 'em. I called the extension agent here in the county—Denny Carlton's his name—and asked him about it." She laughed again. "He didn't believe me 'til he came out here early one morning to see for himself. He got out of his car and just stood there with his mouth hanging open. He believed me then, especially when he had to push 'em out of his way to get to the front door."

I shuddered at the thought. "Why did they come here?"

"Don't know why they chose this particular place. Denny said that they were migratory birds, probably on their way back up north somewhere and just picked my house as one of their stops.

"They stayed here for the better part of two weeks. Then one morning, they were just gone. And Lord, what an unholy mess they left behind! Took me ages to get rid of all of it. And my car...you wouldn't believe how many times I had to get it washed before it was clean again."

She drained the last of the tea from her cup, then went on. "But while the buzzards were here, people from all over started driving out to see 'em. I guess that's when folks started talking about me. Some thought it was some kind of omen about the end of the world. Others figured it meant I was about to die. But I didn't die, of course, and people started claiming the birds were protecting me. What with those buzzards, and the herbs I grow, they decided I was some kind of witch.

"I didn't know nothing about it until I was in town grocery shopping one day and this shy little girl at the checkout counter told me she was having boyfriend troubles and asked if I could make her a magic bag like the one I had by my front door." She chuckled. "It's not magic, you know, just a mesh bag I filled with some herbs to keep the flies away. But she seemed so pitiful. She wasn't a pretty thing, had acne on her face, stringy hair and looked like she'd run if you said boo to her. I told her I would, just 'cause I thought it might make her feel better about things. And the next time I went to town I took her a little bag full of herbs. You'da thought I'd brought her a bag of money, she was so grateful. Tried to pay me for it, but I wouldn't take anything."

"What about the hooligans?"

She grinned. "Oh, yeah. That was something. One night right after the buzzards came, a carload of those boys came out here. I'm sure they were up to some mischief or other. They musta parked their car down the road a ways, planning to sneak up on the house. But they didn't know about the buzzards. I guess the birds were surprised, too. All of a sudden there was this squawking and terrible screaming from the yard.

"By the time I got to the door and switched on the porch light, all I could see was black wings flapping everywhere and those boys were yelling and trying to get away. One of 'em was trying to crawl his way out of the yard." She gave a deep laugh. "Funniest thing I ever saw.

"So, with that and the little girl in town, word about me being a witch started getting around and I've let it. Can't see the harm in it really. A couple of times a week folks come to my door asking me for help. And you better believe I've never had any more young vandals come calling."

"What do you do for the people who come to you?"

"Well, if they're sick I send 'em on to the doctor, but most of 'em are just looking for something to fix the problems they're having in their lives—with husbands or boyfriends, mostly. A few are trying to get ahead in business of some kind."

A frown creased her forehead. "They just need someone to tell 'em the truth and give 'em some sensible advice, but they wouldn't take it if you just told 'em. So I mix a little herb lore and a little magic nonsense in with the advice and off they go. I believe I actually help some people. I even let 'em pay me a few dollars. Folks don't value things 'less they cost 'em something."

We were quiet for a moment. My eyes fell on the frog display.

"I see you're a collector."

She glanced at the frogs and gave a laugh. "Not really. When I moved here I had a few of those little things. Bill and I picked 'em up in different places over the years. But people would come see me and notice the frogs and word got around that I collected them. Now it seems like everybody that comes here brings me another one. They like to give the witch presents, I guess."

She gently dislodged the cat from her lap and got us both another cup of tea. The rain had started again, harder this time, and I could hear it against the windows. I said a quick prayer of thanks that I was warm and sheltered.

When Miss Gene had stirred the fire some more and was comfortably settled back in her chair, she told me about Jim and Robin Lazenby.

"Folks tell me things that they wouldn't tell anybody else. So, even living out here in the middle of nowhere, I got a pretty good idea 'bout what's going on in Ben Hill County. And I've had an earful about Jim Lazenby."

The cat climbed back into her lap and Miss Gene stroked the

black fur. "Now the first thing you need to know is that Jim Lazen-by'll do anything to get ahead. He doesn't care about anyone or any-thing—all he's interested in is making money and being a big man. Nobody wants to get between him and what he wants." She raised an eyebrow. "Looks like that's what you tried to do this afternoon."

"It seems like a pretty damned extreme reaction to me asking for the Coopers' money back."

"Well, he's made 'bout all the money there is to make in Fitzger-ald. He's vice president of the Chamber of Commerce and a big man in the country club set. Now he's set his sights on something more than that. He's planning to run for state senate next year, supposed to be announcing that come January or February. He's already lined up Jamie Arthur as his campaign chairman. Jim's a natural-born politician, a charming devil, if you don't know him too well. He'll probably get elected.

"He's sure working on it. He's on every charitable committee in town. He and his wife entertain all the best people. It's like he never stops. He's in church every time the doors open and on those evenings he doesn't have some meeting or other, he's in the bar at Carlo's Restaurant, shaking hands and talking to anybody who hap-pens to be there."

"It sounds like he's doing all the right stuff," I said.

She nodded in agreement. "Only thing that might stop him is if people find out 'bout some of the things in his past—and there's some ugly stuff. He'll do whatever it takes to make sure that doesn't happen."

"Things like him taking the Coopers' money?"

"That and other things."

"Like what?"

She pursed her lips. "Well, there's murder."

ELEVEN

SINCE DANNY COOPER HAD ALREADY TOLD ME ABOUT THE death of Lazenby's former partner, I wasn't exactly surprised when Miss Gene mentioned Franklin Eckley.

"Jim Lazenby killed that man and you can take *that* fact to the bank."

"How do you know?"

She straightened a bit in her chair. "I've known the Eckley family for years. Franklin's sister Amy has been coming out to see me since she and her husband got divorced back in '08. Poor little thing. Her husband had been foolin' around with Jinny Rachels down at the Piggly Wiggly. Amy thought she wanted a potion to get him back, but what she really needed was some backbone to start being her own person."

I was fascinated by how Miss Gene conducted her business. "And you helped her with that?"

"Well, she did the work herself. I just kinda guided her along." She chuckled. "See, I wrapped up some herbs and a couple of pebbles in a little bag and tied it with a red ribbon. Told her she had to keep it with her all the time and, if it was going to work, she had to follow some strict rules. She wasn't allowed to call him or write to him or even see him. If she ran into him anywhere, she was to turn and leave. I told her she wasn't even allowed to think about him. And if she could do all that for three months, everything would work out fine."

The warmth and the day I'd had were combining to make me sleepy. I sat up straighter in my chair, hoping to feel more alert. "So what happened?"

"Well, she'd been driving him near crazy with all her phone calls, beggin' him to come home. When she stopped all of a sudden, he was curious. Then he got downright concerned. He'd got so used to her being there, waiting for him, that he didn't know what to do. *He* started calling *her*—and she wouldn't even talk to him. Just said 'I can't talk to you' and hung up.

"And since she wasn't spending all that time trying to get him back, little Amy had to find something else to occupy her time. She started going to the Methodist church and even joined the choir. And she started volunteering over at the hospital. She made some new friends. After two months had passed, her no good husband came crawling home, begging her to take him back."

Her eyes were bright as she waited a few seconds to deliver the punch line. "But you know what? She wouldn't do it! She'd found out she could get along without him just fine. And that's how that spell worked."

I laughed along with her, but then went back to our original subject. "So that's how you learned about Franklin Eckley being killed?"

"Yes, in a roundabout sorta way. Amy always talked a lot about her baby brother Frankie. He was the apple of her eye. He was a quiet boy growing up, usually had his nose in a book. Good student, parents never had a single day of trouble from him. He went off to college, but came right back here after he graduated, married and opened his own business. He was an accountant, a whatayacallit, a CPA. He was doing really good 'til he got mixed up with that Lazenby fellow.

"All of a sudden poor Frankie—the nice guy that bought his clothes at Belk and whose wife clipped coupons from the paper every Sunday—started believing that he was going to be some kind of real estate millionaire. Him and Lazenby bought a big piece of land out on Ashburn Highway and started laying out the plan to this fancy subdivision. They were going to call it Lazenby Acres 'cause Jim owned 51% of the project and got to name it. But Amy said Frankie was okay with that. The main street was going to be called Eckley Boulevard. And, oh, the houses were going to be these brick mansion-looking things. It was gonna be wonderful—they thought."

Thunder rumbled in the distance, but Miss Gene paid no attention to it.

"But then the money started running low. They'd spent a lot, I guess, on the land itself and having it graded and the streets put in and all. And they owed more money than either of 'em had. So there they were with all the streets and empty lots and nothing leftover to build even a few houses for folks to come and see. You know, contractors have to be paid regular so they can pay *their* workers. They weren't interested in working for promises. And nobody was gonna buy a house sight unseen."

"I'm sure the recession didn't help."

"Yes, that was the final nail in the coffin, I guess you could say. Everybody thought both of 'em were going to lose everything they had. Things were getting desperate until December, five or six years ago."

"What happened?"

"Frankie and Lazenby had been out at the property, meeting with a new contractor, trying to work something out to get at least one house built. It was late in the day—and you know how it gets dark so early in December? Must have been almost six when they left. Lazenby told the police later that he and the contractor left about the same time, that Frankie was sitting in his car talking on his phone and should have only been a couple of minutes behind them."

She shook her head. "It was so sad. They didn't find him 'til the next morning. Car had run off the road and into a tree. The people who investigated the accident said the tire marks and stuff proved he was going over 70 miles an hour, said he musta swerved to miss a deer. There's deer everywhere around here."

The story made me shudder. If I'd been killed, would the official verdict have been that I, like Eckley, had swerved to miss a deer? I wondered if the "deer" I encountered was the same one that did in Eckley. "I gather you don't think that's what happened?"

She snorted. "Me and half the town. I mean, it was real convenient for Jim Lazenby. When they'd started the project, him and Frankie each took out insurance policies that would pay the other if they died. Survivor insurance, pretty common in business partnerships. Anyhow, Frankie's policy paid off—two million dollars was what I heard—and Lazenby was able to take care of all their debts with some to spare."

"Did he go ahead and build the subdivision?"

"No, wasn't enough money for *that*. The land's still sitting out there, all overgrown with weeds, still waiting for the first house. But Lazenby got out okay." She gave me a level look. "Nobody will ever convince me that poor Frankie died like they said. He'd been driving these roads all his life. He'd know better than to speed along at nightfall when the deer are moving about. No, somebody was chasing him. And they run him off the road. That's what happened, no matter what the official verdict was."

Over the next hour, Miss Gene told me everything she knew about Jim and Robin Lazenby. Although his real estate business was moderately successful, most of his money came from rental property. He was something of a local legend in Ben Hill County. Just like Stacy Cooper told me, on the first of every month, he climbed into his big Lexus LS and made the rounds. Between three and seven in the afternoon, he visited every house he owned and personally collected the rent for the coming month.

"He always wants his money in cash," Miss Gene said. "And God help them that don't have it. He'll foreclose on 'em in a New York minute,"

Danny Cooper had mentioned Lazenby's penchant for cash as well.

"I'd guess not all of that money gets reported to Uncle Sam," Miss Gene said. I agreed with her.

"He's just a mean, greedy man," she said. Then she raised her eyebrows and said, "But he's not mean to everyone—at least, not all the time."

Lazenby, she told me, had had a string of women over the years. "He likes all kinds, but he's especially partial to those that are as different as possible from his wife. Guess he thinks plain old local women are boring. Last year there was talk about him and a lady veterinarian over in Cordele. Heard she was from Pakistan or some place like that. Year before that he hooked up with a high school teacher who moved here from New York.

"Right now, he's paying the rent on a little duplex for his receptionist, Cheryl Pressley. She moved here from California about ten years ago when her mama got a job teaching at the high school." She sighed. "And rumor has it that he's got her pregnant." I remembered the gorgeous young woman in Lazenby's office that afternoon. "She's a smart girl, could have had a bright future. Now, she'll probably end up leaving town and raising the baby on her own. It's not the first time and I guess it won't be the last."

"How does his wife handle that?"

Miss Gene sighed. "Poor Robin. She married him 'cause he was a football hero and, maybe, 'cause her daddy was so against it. It took her a while to realize what Jim really was. But by then they had the two children and Robin couldn't admit her mistake. Pride's a terrible thing. So she's still with him, putting on a good face.

"She used to come to see me some, trying to find a way to make Jim fall back in love with her. She even tried to get pregnant again—thought that might bring him back—but she had had two miscarriages and finally gave that up."

"She doesn't come anymore?"

Miss Gene shook her head. "No. Didn't want to listen to my advice—which was to get out of that marriage. Last time I talked to her she'd decided there might be some kind of curse on him. I didn't have the heart to tell her that he's just a snake—always has been. I did what I could to help her, tried to guide her away from him, but it didn't do any good. I believe she'd like to leave, but she's scared." She frowned. "And maybe Jim's given her something to be scared about over the years. I can't say for sure, but she's always acted kinda wary, you know, like she's afraid she might get hurt.

"Now a lot of the time, it's like Robin isn't there anymore. Rumor is she drinks and maybe does worse. She's a mess. She's embarrassed her kids so many times that they both avoid spending any time with her. I heard she was caught shoplifting in WalMart last summer up in Cordele or Macon or somewhere."

"Was she arrested?"

"No. Jim got it all hushed up somehow. And after that she was in a rehab hospital in Atlanta, although they told everybody she was spending a month touring Europe. She's been a little quieter since then, I guess. There haven't been any more scenes or anything. Maybe it worked.

"Or maybe it's all that magic stuff." She smiled without humor. "When I couldn't help her with good advice and a little bag, she looked around for something more dramatic—spells or magic potions or something. Anyway, she hasn't been out here in a couple of years and now she's got this store over on Sherman Street where she sells crystals and tarot cards and those little sticks you throw to tell your fortune, can't remember what they're called. If they make it and call it magic, Robin's got it." She smiled. "Guess you could say she's my competition."

"Does she really believe all that stuff?"

Miss Gene shrugged. "Don't know. I think she'd like to. She's looking for something to fix her life, something to make her happy again. 'Course, getting rid of that rotten husband would do it pretty quick, but she won't hear of that."

It was nearly ten and I could barely keep my eyes opened. Miss Gene got me settled in a small bedroom and said good night. I unwrapped my knee, thinking I'd be more comfortable. Then, still in the robe, climbed between the covers of the iron bedstead.

I think I was asleep before my head sank into the pillow, but it wasn't a restful night. Curled up under Miss Gene's old quilt, I dreamed over and over about the crash. I'd wake, heart racing, only to fall back asleep and encounter the same terrifying images again. When daylight lit the room just after seven, I knew I wasn't going to sleep any more, even though I felt almost more tired than I had the night before.

TWELVE

GETTING OUT OF BED WAS A PAINFUL PROCESS. MY KNEE WAS twice its usual size and hurt like the devil when any weight was put on it. I carefully rewrapped it, dressed in yesterday's clothes — dried now, but wrinkled — and hobbled into the kitchen.

"Good morning," Miss Gene said.

I mumbled a greeting and painfully lowered myself into a seat at the table. She gave me a cup of coffee.

"Looks like that knee is really hurting." She put a bottle of Tylenol and a glass of water in front of me. "Take three of 'em. Won't hurt you and it might help."

I gave her a puzzled look and she laughed. "What? You think a witch oughta be givin' you a potion or something? Honey, that knee is wrenched bad. You need a good anti-inflammatory and a doctor."

I gulped the pills down and Miss Gene took a pan of biscuits out of the oven. We feasted on biscuits and sausage gravy, then got on with everything that had to be done.

Miss Gene let me use her phone to call Linda Winkler. I told her I'd been in an accident.

"I'm fine," I said, over her words of concern, "but I had to stay here overnight. Can you go by the house and give the cat some fresh food and water? The food is in the pantry."

Linda and I had always had keys to each other's houses.

"No problem, sweetie. I'll take care of it. But I don't plan to try and pet that animal again until he's learned some social skills."

Next I called the local police and by 8:30 a sheriff's deputy named Jenkins was sitting in Miss Gene's living room, taking a report. I told him everything that had happened.

"So you think Jim Lazenby ran you off the road and chased you through the woods?" He sounded skeptical.

"No, I don't. Lazenby wasn't the man who wrecked me. But I think he was responsible."

"Could you identify the man who did it?"

"I doubt it. I never really saw his face close up." I thought back to how my attacker looked watching me from the road. "He was white with dark hair. He looked big and he was wearing jeans and a long-sleeved navy blue tee shirt." I shrugged. "That's all I can give you."

My description of the truck wasn't any better. It was gray and mid-sized. I thought it might have been a Chevrolet, but wasn't sure. I knew I'd provided next to nothing to go on.

He shook his head. "Well, I'll put in the report and I guess somebody'll go talk to Lazenby, but without more …"

"I know, I know. I don't expect anything to come from it. I just wanted the incident to be on record. I appreciate you taking the report."

I thanked Miss Gene for all her help and she gave me a hug.

"Now don't be a stranger, honey. You come back and see me soon."

The day was cool and overcast and fog lay in the low spots. Deputy Jenkins drove me back to where the Trailblazer lay crumpled and lopsided in the woods beside the highway.

"No wonder nobody called it in overnight," he said as we got out of his car. "You can hardly see it even when you're looking for it."

The deputy climbed down the slope to the edge of the wooded area and slowly circled the wreck. I stayed up on the road, unwilling to risk further injury to my knee. Jenkins shook his head several times and I gathered the prognosis for the vehicle wasn't good. Before he came back to the cruiser, he reached into the SUV and retrieved my handbag.

"Your phone was on the floor and I put it in your purse for you. I'd have brought those papers back, too, but they're scattered all over the place."

I thanked him, grateful that my bag had a nice secure zipper. My wallet, complete with credit cards and cash were all there.

Two hours later, the Trailblazer had been hauled into town and deposited at a local garage. The proprietor's opinion was that it was totaled.

"I'd say that it's toast," was the way he put it.

I reported the wreck to my insurance company, then arranged for a rental car. The last thing I did before leaving Fitzgerald was climb into the mangled Trailblazer and retrieve the information I'd accumulated on Lazenby. The papers were strewn everywhere, It took some time and painful scrambling, but I got finally got them all.

The pain from my knee and other assorted bumps and bruises never let up, but anger kept me going on the rainy drive home. I knew Lazenby was to blame for this and, one way or another, he was going to pay for it.

At 4:15, I let myself into the house. I was piling my things on the kitchen table when I noticed a couple of baskets in the middle of the floor.

"What in the world ..."

Then my eyes went up. I used the tops of the kitchen cabinets as storage space for bulky things like seldom-used appliances, oversized kettles... and baskets. Now two of the baskets had been replaced by a cat. Curtis looked down at me and slowly blinked his eyes.

"We're going to have to come to an understanding, cat."

But not now. Now I just wanted to enjoy being home. I took a few minutes to scoop out the cat box and check the food bowl, then went to work on myself.

After a shower, I stood in front of the mirror and surveyed the damage. My arms, hands, neck, and face were a road map of scratches, but they didn't really hurt and I covered up a lot of them with a long-sleeved turtleneck jersey. I rewrapped my knee with a clean Ace bandage and pulled on a loose pair of jeans.

The evening was uneventful and I slept late on Friday. Curtis must have been glad I was back; he was sleeping peacefully on the foot of the bed and hadn't even head butted me for an early breakfast.

When I slipped out of the bed at 9:30, I was surprised that I actually felt better. The soreness was fading a bit and the swelling in my knee was down a lot. After I wrapped it securely, I could almost walk normally. Rain still fell, but I didn't mind. I wasn't going anywhere.

THIRTEEN

BRUNSWICK STEW TAKES A WHILE TO PREPARE. THERE'S A
lot of prep work and it has to cook for hours, but it's worth the
effort. So I spent most of Friday evening in the kitchen. Curtis was
right there with me most of the time. I don't know if he was concerned I might leave again or he simply smelled food and was hoping I'd drop my guard so he could have a shot at it.

By eleven, the stew was in the fridge and I was ready for bed.
Standing all that time in the kitchen had brought back some knee
pain and I filled an icebag. Curtis followed me into the bedroom
and jumped on the bed as if he'd always slept there. I slid between
the covers, positioned the icebag on my knee, and closed my eyes.

Just as I started to drop off, my mind veered to Owen and Sarah
and their big house up on the hill. It was the first time I'd given
them a thought in two days. I wasn't jealous, I swear I wasn't, but I
did think it was tacky of them to move into my neighborhood. And
I wouldn't have minded if their nice, new roof sprang a leak.

The rain ended by morning, leaving behind freshly washed blue
skies and the golden light that we only see in the fall. A glorious
day by anyone's standards. I put Jim Lazenby, the Coopers, and my
ex-husband firmly out of my mind that afternoon and concentrated

instead on three things: my expected guests, whether I could keep the cat from injuring one of them and, of course, football. More specifically, University of Georgia football.

College football isn't just a sport in the South. It's more like a religion — with its own music, rituals, and offerings. And I was preparing to serve as an acolyte in the temple for one of the most important services of the year. At eight that night, Georgia and Tennessee would meet on the battlefield of Neyland Stadium in Knoxville. Both teams were still undefeated and the winner of tonight's game would likely go on to play for the SEC championship.

The Bulldogs had a terrific season going for them. With three games to go and a sophomore running back that people were beginning to compare to the great Herschel Walker, expectations were high. Tennessee was the only ranked opponent they had yet to face.

Three friends were joining me to watch the game. Only one of us was an actual alumnus of the university, but it didn't matter. Tonight, we'd all be Bulldogs, eager to do our part to cheer the team to victory.

Along with the stew and the cornbread which would soon be baking in the oven, there was enough coleslaw and potato salad in the fridge to feed half the neighborhood.

I stacked plates and bowls on the dining room table and, back in the kitchen, helped myself to a beer from the big blue cooler I'd put near the back door. With the fridge jammed, I'd had to find another place for the beer — two six-packs of Fosters and the same amount of Sweet Water Extra Pale Ale, a nice Atlanta-produced brew that went well with spicy food.

As a gesture to my friends who enjoyed such things, I'd pushed a couple of oversized bottles of wine down in the ice, too. There was one bottle of red and one of white. I'd made sure to get the kind with corks and not screw off tops. I didn't know exactly what they were, but the labels were pretty and they didn't cost that much. I'm a beer lover and drinking wine holds about as much interest for me as watching people play poker on television, but I wanted to be hospitable.

It was the wine that caused the problem. I searched every drawer in the kitchen, but finally had to accept the fact that there wasn't a corkscrew in the house. I knew that long ago, when Owen and I were married, we'd had a corkscrew, but evidently he'd gotten custody of it in the divorce.

It was 5:20. There was no time to go buy one. I knew Linda wasn't home. I tried calling Judy Nixon down the street and Marty Berkowitz next door, but didn't get an answer in either place. The McElveys who lived in the house diagonally across from mine were teetotalers and unlikely to possess such a tool. That left only one other place in the cul de sac — Catherine Clooney's old house — now occupied by the guy with the motorcycle.

I weighed my choices — I could try prying out corks with a kitchen knife or go begging to the motorcycle thug. Two minutes later I walked slowly across the street — my knee still not a hundred percent — and rang his doorbell.

"Well, hello there." The man who opened the door didn't look like a thug. In a long-sleeved white polo shirt tucked neatly into very well-fitting jeans, he looked like a GQ model, albeit one of the older ones they featured to demonstrate that all good-looking men didn't have to be in their twenties. He was certainly good looking enough to be a model — with vivid blue eyes and a smile that made you want to smile right back at him. I guessed his age as late 50's, not so much because of the gray scattered through his longish dark hair as the subdivision's age requirements.

"I...I'm Emily Christopher. I live across the street."

"Pleased to meet you, Emily. I'm Nick Buckley." I shook the hand he extended. He must have noticed the scratches on my face, but was too polite to mention them. "Come in. Can I offer you coffee or a drink?"

I stepped into the entry way. In the room beyond there were pieces of furniture that looked as if they hadn't yet found their proper places. Boxes stacked here and there emphasized that moving in was still in progress.

"No, no, thank you. I was...uh...wondering if you might have a corkscrew I could borrow? I have some friends coming over to watch the game and can't find mine."

"Sure do."

I followed him into the kitchen where I was surprised to see a new stainless steel pot rack suspended from the ceiling above the island. Two skillets and several saucepans dangled from it.

"Nice pot rack," I said.

He looked up from the drawer he'd opened. "Oh, yeah, it is. Had to do something to add storage space. Ah, here it is." He handed me the requested tool. "So, you're going to watch the Georgia game? Me, too. Never miss the Dogs if I can help it."

He grinned and, before I could even consider why I did it, I asked, "Are you going to be watching alone?"

"Yeah. Thought maybe I'd order a pizza."

"Why don't you come over and watch it with me and my friends? We'll have plenty of food."

He didn't even hesitate. "I'd love to. It's always more fun that way."

"Okay. About 6:00 then."

Walking home, I wondered what had possessed me to invite a total stranger to dinner. I didn't know anything about him. Maybe he was a drunk or a bigot or crazy as a loon. I tried telling myself I was just being neighborly, but had to admit that wasn't it. It was those eyes... and maybe the jeans.

By six, everything, including the hostess, was ready. I'd showered, blown my hair dry and even applied eyeliner and mascara. I'd considered trying to cover the scratches with makeup, but decided it would just look like a bad paint job. Corduroy slacks and a soft blue cotton sweater nicely covered the rest of the damages and felt just right for an autumn evening. I could even walk without a limp if I was careful.

My nephew Michael Engelsen, known as Mico, was the first to arrive. His partner Eben Rivers followed him in the door.

"Emily, precious!" Mico managed to plant an awkward kiss on my cheek over the large pot he carried. Then he pulled back and his eyes narrowed as he got a good look at my face. "What in the world happened to you?"

"Just a little accident. I'll tell you all about it later. What have you got there?"

He raised the pot a few inches. "It's vegetarian chili. Since you insist on catering to carnivores, we decided it might be wise to bring our own food."

"Just put it on the stove." I turned to his companion. "Hey, Eben. Good to see you."

Eben gave me a shy smile. They were a new couple, but seemed well suited to each other. Mico, tall, blond and relentlessly outgoing as befitted a successful art dealer, was a nice counterpart to the quiet, slightly built man with milk-pale skin and dark eyes and hair. A local veterinarian, Eben had brought vegetarianism into Mico's life. I didn't know him well, but I'd never seen Mico so happy. I'd tolerate vegetarian chili any day for that.

"You guys grab a beer or some wine," I gestured toward the cooler, "and get comfortable."

Both chose beer. Mico leaned back against the counter, took a swallow from his bottle and looked around admiringly. "I like this house more every time I see it. And what a change!" He gave me a big grin. "Although I sort of miss the dank, cave-like ambience of your old apartment. Such a mysterious atmosphere—you never knew what might be hiding in the dark recesses of those closets and cabinets."

After Owen and I divorced, we sold our big family home and I'd moved into a small apartment while I decided where I wanted to live permanently.

I laughed. "Isn't it wonderful? I've never lived in a brand-new house before. It's strange not having something break every other week."

"Sounds like heaven. My place is so old that something's always going wrong," Mico said. Twelve years before, he'd bought a big Victorian in Atlanta's Inman Park and lovingly restored it. "Just yesterday I had to put a new faucet in the bathroom and I'm pretty sure the dishwasher isn't long for this world either. What I wouldn't give for a new house."

Eben smiled. "I hear you complaining, but you can't convince me you'd ever move." He gave me a conspiratorial look. "He loves that monstrosity. The only way he'll leave it is feet first."

Mico gave a laugh. "Then I guess you're stuck with it, too."

The two exchanged smiles. "Guess so," Eben said. He didn't sound unhappy about the idea.

Annette Thibidoux arrived about then, joining us in the kitchen. She, too, gave my face a long look. "Honey, what have you *done* to yourself?"

"A minor accident. Nothing serious." I knew I'd have to explain what happened eventually, but right now getting dinner served was more important. I nodded toward the covered baking dish Annette held. "What have you got there?"

"Crabmeat-stuffed mushrooms. Just need to pop them in the oven for a few minutes before you serve them."

They'd be delicious, I knew. She'd brought the same dish to the District Attorney's Office Christmas party last year and they'd disappeared almost before she set them on the table.

Annette was a good twenty years younger than I was and the best investigator I'd ever met. When I'd worked full time in the DA's Office full time, we were a good team. Now that I was a part-time consultant, she was technically my boss.

The only way to describe Annette was spectacular — six feet tall, with the body of a personal trainer and the face of an angel. Dressed tonight in an orange and red silk caftan, with a cascade of braids down her back, she looked like one of the African queens from whom she was surely descended.

"I thought you might bring Derek tonight." I'd only met him once back in February, but he'd seemed nice enough.

She sniffed. "Not likely. Derek is a thing of the past."

That wasn't a big surprise. I wondered what he'd done to be scratched off Annette's list. It didn't have to be too serious a misdeed. She changed men like most women did shoes, enjoying them when they were new, but tossing them aside after they got a little wear on them. And she never seemed to run out of a fresh supply.

After the mushrooms were safely deposited on a counter top, she pulled a corkscrew and a bottle of wine from her shoulder tote.

"Oh, I should have told you. I've got wine tonight," I told her. "Two bottles. They're in the cooler. And I've got a corkscrew, too."

She lifted the lid, gave my iced-down wines a quick look and smiled at me. "I'm sure they're fine," she said, using the same tone you would with a small child who's just offered you a mud pie, "but I'm kind of used to this brand. I believe I'll just drink it."

She deftly removed the cork and poured herself a generous glass of the deep red wine. "You know, every time I come up here, I like this neighborhood more. That park down the block is so pretty. And everybody on the streets smiles and waves." She sipped her wine. "I might just have to move in here myself."

"I don't think the HOA would allow that. You're a little too young."

"Oh, yeah." She grinned. "I almost forgot this was an old timers' community."

My guests had moved into the living room and turned on the TV, volume down, by the time Nick Buckley rang the bell. The house seemed smaller as soon as he entered. He brought a tray with a bowl of pale green dip surrounded by fresh vegetables.

The others came to meet him and I made introductions as I set the tray on the dining room table. Mico was the first to sample the dip. Being vegetarian didn't mean he avoided dairy.

"That's really good," he said approvingly. "What is it?"

"Goat cheese, sour cream, and fresh herbs."

Mico nodded and I knew the mixture would soon find a place in his repertoire.

Nick took a chair in the living room and didn't seem to mind a bit answering the questions the others asked. A newcomer to our group was a novelty. We learned that Nick was a real estate developer, working mostly on industrial projects.

"But I'm almost retired," he explained. "My son handles most of the day to day stuff. Now I only get involved in things that interest me."

"So what interests you?" Annette asked.

"We're just starting a development in Portugal — residential and commercial — that's going to be 80% solar powered. Fascinating concept. I'll be spending quite a bit of time over there. In fact, I'm leaving for a couple of weeks later this month."

I went to check on the food and took a minute to look around for the cat. I didn't see him. He must have hidden as soon as the first guest entered the house. He wasn't a sociable sort, but at least he hadn't scratched anyone.

Annette joined me in the kitchen a minute later. "Where did you find that *gorgeous* man?"

"He's my neighbor. Just met him this afternoon when I went over to borrow a corkscrew." I raised an eyebrow at her. "Which I wouldn't have had to do if I'd known you were bringing your own."

"I'm glad you did. It gave you an excuse to invite the hunk."

"I just invited him to be polite. I mean, once I mentioned the game and he said he was watching it alone..."

"Sure," she said with an exaggerated nod. "You were just being neighborly. You'd have done the same thing if he'd been a three-foot tall, balding troll, right?"

FOURTEEN

BY KICK OFF, WE WERE ALL GATHERED AROUND THE TV. A
significant dent had been made in both the Brunswick stew and the
chili; there wasn't much dip left and not a single mushroom had
survived.

At exactly 8:20 the game began. We shouted and screamed as if
we were right there in the stadium. I was pleased that everyone had
their priorities straight—you watch the action and carry on your
conversations during the commercials. Nick fit right in. You'd have
thought he'd known everyone for years instead of hours.

During halftime, we went back for seconds on the food.

"Okay, Emily," Mico said around a mouthful of cornbread.
"You've put it off long enough. What happened to you? And don't
give me that 'little accident' crap again."

I sighed. "Okay. But I have to start with Catherine Clooney's
will."

"Who?" Annette asked.

"A neighbor who died recently." I nodded at Nick. "You just
moved into her house."

"I thought the name Clooney sounded familiar."

I told them about Catherine's will. "She wanted me to get back her great grandson's $8,000. He was swindled out of it in a nasty little lease-purchase scam by a man named Jim Lazenby." I took a bite of the chili. Vegetarian or not, it was delicious.

"Wow," Annette said. "That's some favor to ask! And from beyond the grave, too. Hard to say no." She tilted her head a bit. "So how are you going to get the money back?"

"I don't understand. Why would she think *you* could help with something like that?" Nick asked.

I reached for my beer and took a sip. "I used to be in law enforcement."

"And she still works with me at the DA's Office," Annette put in.

Nick looked at me with a bit of surprise, but only asked, "So how *are* you going to do it?"

"Well, I started looking into it this week. Drove down to Fitzgerald, met with the Coopers, and then with Lazenby himself." I gave a mirthless laugh. "I thought maybe I could convince him to give the money back. You know, out of the goodness of his heart. But I don't think he's got a heart. And he's totally lacking in goodness. The only thing I accomplished was to get run off the road by a thug in a pickup."

"Oh, my God," Mico said leaning toward me. "Were you hurt? I mean, I can see your face, but ..."

"Just some bruises and bumps, but the car was totaled. I got the scratches running away from him in the woods. I'm sure Lazenby expected me to be killed—from what I've heard it wouldn't be the first time that happened to someone he didn't like."

"That's a pretty damned extreme reaction to disliking someone," Annette said.

"I agree. And it was unnecessary," I said. "All I ever planned to do was talk to him and snoop around a little to make sure no legal recourse for the Coopers had been overlooked. I didn't really expect to find anything. In fact, I'd already planned to send the money Catherine left me to her grandson and be done with it. But now ... something has to be done about this man."

"This Lazenby, the one who ran you off the road, was he arrested?" Annette asked. "Is he still in jail?"

"No, no one's in jail. I reported it, of course. I couldn't identify the driver, but I saw enough of him to know it wasn't Lazenby himself. I don't have any doubt he sent the guy in the truck, but there's no way to prove it."

"If the police can't touch him, what can you do?" Mico asked.

"I'm not sure just yet. I've got to think about it some more." A few leaves rustled on the plant in the corner. "Oh, yeah, Catherine left me her cat, too."

"She left you a cat?" Annette asked, looking around. "Where is it?"

I pointed to the multi-colored croton in the corner near the patio door. "Behind the plant. I guess he's been there all evening. He's started to warm up with me, but he's not very good with strangers."

Eben crossed the room and looked behind the plant.

"He's frightened, of course. He's in unfamiliar territory with people he doesn't know. It'll take him some time to adjust." Eben wasn't shy now that he was in professional mode. "Was he an outside or an inside cat?"

"Inside. In the instructions she left me, Catherine said he shouldn't go outside."

He squatted down beside the cat.

"Be careful," I warned. "He almost took off Linda's hand."

93

"Ummm." He ran a hand down Curtis's back. I held my breath, but the cat didn't show any hostility. "Well, he looks to be healthy."

"I guess so. I haven't had time to check his records." I rolled my eyes. "I still can't believe she kept all his medical records."

"She did?" He was really interested now. "May I see them?"

"Uh, sure."

I fetched the papers from my desk and handed them to him as he sat back down. The second half was starting. In between plays, Eben read through the papers. Sometime during the fourth quarter, he went over and picked up Curtis, who didn't resist at all. In fact, he snuggled up to next to Eben on the sofa while the vet ran his hands over his fur.

"He's about two years old," Eben told me during a commercial, "and he's current on all his vaccines."

"Well, that's one less thing to worry about," I said.

Curtis didn't even look at me—the one who'd given him a home, food and, of course, that litter box. Instead he climbed into Eben's lap and went to sleep.

The Bulldogs were dead on that night, even in front of more than 100,000 screaming Tennessee fans. Although the lead changed hands a few times, Georgia took the win in the end. Everyone in the room felt we'd earned a part in the victory celebration.

Although the game was over and the food just about gone, no one made any move to leave. While Eben and the newly-sociable Curtis sprawled on the sofa watching the post-game show, Mico and Nick picked up plates and glasses and brought them into the kitchen where Annette scraped and rinsed the plates. She handed them to me and I loaded the dishwasher.

Nick was right at home in my kitchen, putting things in their proper places as if he'd done it a hundred times. And when he reached past me to put silverware in the sink, his arm left behind an unsettling warmth as it grazed mine.

"Exactly how did this Lazenby character get the Coopers' money?" he asked.

I explained the lease-purchase agreement that Lazenby had used it to take advantage of the young couple. "And they aren't the only ones he's duped out of their down payment. There are others — don't know how many — but enough that it's pretty common knowledge down in Fitzgerald."

Nick nodded. "Sad to say, I've heard of that happening before. People are so anxious to buy their own homes that they jump in with both feet. They don't take the time to review everything."

"In this case, their big mistake was trusting Jim Lazenby."

"He shouldn't be allowed to get away with something like that," Eben said, bringing his empty bowl into the kitchen.

Annette leaned back against the counter top, arms crossed. "This world can be a treacherous place. People'll screw you six ways to Sunday and smile while they're doing it."

"From what I learned, Lazenby is a dangerous guy." I told them about Franklin Eckley. "But there wasn't any way to prove his death was anything other than an accident."

"I guess you're right if you say there's no legal way to help the Coopers," Mico said. "You know more about that stuff than I do. But I can't believe that there's nothing that can be done to help those kids or to stop this guy. Surely there's something." He gestured, spreading both hands out in front of him. "I'd be glad to help if there's anything I can do. You know, a little paying it forward."

He sat up straighter, warming to his idea. "Hey, even if we

can't get the money back, maybe we could do some fundraising or take up a collection or something." He gave Eben a quick smile. "Don't think there's anyone here who couldn't use a little positive karma."

I gave him a look to let him know how much stock I put in karma. "Let's put that on hold for right now. I need to do some thinking."

"Well, you wouldn't mind if I did some research on this Lazenby guy, would it?" Annette asked. I'd already done what I could, but I knew she was way ahead of me in that department. If there was anything I'd missed about Lazenby out there in cyberspace, she'd find it. "Just give me his stats before I leave."

A few minutes later, Annette was out the door. "I'll let you know what I find on Lazenby." I knew she'd be at her computer as soon as she got home. The woman loved a mission.

"It's not urgent enough to call me in the middle of the night," I cautioned. "Tomorrow or the next day is fine."

Mico and Eben followed soon after Annette, but Nick stayed behind, nursing a last beer. It was almost midnight.

"Thanks for including me," he said. He leaned back in the chair, stretching out the kinks. My kitchen chairs weren't especially comfortable. "I really like your friends."

"They liked you, too. I could tell. And I'm glad you enjoyed the evening."

"Yeah, I did." He got to his feet, then walked over and pulled the overloaded plastic bag from the kitchen garbage can and tied the end. "This is pretty heavy. I'll leave it on the curb on my way home."

I laughed. "Easy to see that you're new to Marchpoint. We'll have to try and stuff it in the can in the garage. Garbage pick-up isn't until Monday and nothing goes on the curb until Sunday night. If I put a bag out tonight, Milt the Snitch will turn me in."

"Who?"

"Milton Overton," I told him with a smile. "He's a widower, lives down on Mountain Brook. He has a golf cart and an overdeveloped sense of civic duty. You can't miss him—he patrols the entire neighborhood every day, making notes of any covenant violations he finds. And every single week, he writes up a report to the HOA."

"You're not serious."

"Oh, yes, I am. Milton's a legend around here. People think he's a little crazy, but he does keep us all honest."

Shaking his head, Nick carried the bag into the garage and I followed, hitting the button. As the door rose, cold air flooded in. He swung the bag into the already full garbage container. It stuck up several inches above the top, keeping the lid from closing.

"That'll have to do," he said. "I don't think you can cram another thing in there."

"It's fine. I'll put it out tomorrow night." Beyond the door, the cul de sac was deserted. "Well, goodnight."

He put two fingers under my chin, leaned down and kissed me sweetly on the lips. "Goodnight."

Nick was halfway down the drive before I recovered from the surprise.

I was tired enough that I should have slept well Saturday night, but I didn't. The problem with Lazenby wouldn't stop circling in my brain. There had to be some way to bring him down and get the Coopers' money back, but I wasn't smart enough to see it. The few ideas I did come up with as I tossed and turned were ineffective to the point of being silly.

And when I wasn't trying to come up with a solution for the Coopers, my thoughts kept buzzing around Nick Buckley and that kiss. It was after three before sleep mercifully closed down the carnival in my head.

FIFTEEN

I FOLLOWED MY USUAL SUNDAY ROUTINE THE NEXT MORNING, starting with a shower, but Nick still lingered in the back of my consciousness. That kiss hadn't been neighborly. It was definitely more than a thank you for dinner and I wasn't sure how I felt about that.

Owen and I had divorced four years ago and he'd pretty much soured me on the male half of the species. I hadn't been involved with a man since and wasn't sure I ever wanted to be. Romance was way down on my list of things I wanted to do, right below IRS audits and root canals.

Drying off, I regarded myself in the mirror, trying for impartiality, but failing. There were wrinkles and a bit of sagging. Nothing to be done for that, I guessed. And no amount of walking, biking, or swimming can reverse the clock. Still, I was okay with how I looked. Slim, moderately muscular, with green eyes and thick, chin-length graying hair. I didn't mind the gray. I liked to think of it as nature's highlighting.

My face was okay, at least when I smiled—that took away most of the sagging, although it emphasized the wrinkles. At 57, I didn't expect to look or feel 25. But what would a man expect? I shook my head at the stupid thought and got on with the day.

One bright spot that morning was discovering that the swelling was nearly gone from my knee. I thought I might be up to some exercise later in the day.

After breakfast, I settled in a comfortable chair with coffee and the morning paper. Yes, I'm one of the dinosaurs that prefers to hold a newspaper rather than an electronic device in my hand.

Curtis found a square of sunlight beside the living room window, stretched out, and went to sleep. He looked so relaxed that I felt a little guilty. I knew I should be thinking about what I was going to do with him, but finding him another home was going to have to wait until I had some time to devote to the search.

Nick roared out of the neighborhood on his bike about noon. Around 3:00, I wheeled my own bike—pedal-powered, not motorized—out of the garage, donned a helmet, and took off for a leisurely ride around the neighborhood. I wasn't going to push it today. If my knee, which I'd securely wrapped, started to hurt at all, I'd stop.

During the long Georgia summer, the sun was a blistering menace. But now with the November chill in the wind, it was a welcome warmth on my shoulders.

Marchpoint is nestled in the rolling foothills of the Appalachians. It's an area of remarkable beauty, but a fairly challenging terrain for a bicycle. The curving neighborhood streets were constructed on a series of hills, so that bike riding here was made up of two phases: the wheeee! downhill phase and the gasping uphill treks. Out of consideration for my knee, I chose a route that avoided the steeper climbs.

As I pedaled through the Arbor section, I hoped I wouldn't run into Owen or Sarah, and my luck held. The only person I saw on

Spinner Ridge that afternoon was Tilda Earle. She was a compact little woman with tight white curls and a ready smile. She stopped planting bulbs beside her from walk to wave me down. Renowned for her energy, she was active in the Marchpoint Garden Club. But she didn't want to talk gardening today.

"Have you heard about the flasher?" she asked, eyes bright with excitement.

I stopped the bike and put my feet on the ground. "What flasher?"

"You don't know? Then I'm glad I can warn you."

"About a *flasher*?"

"Yes!" she told me. "Marta Schmidt saw him running across her backyard Tuesday afternoon—he was going toward the walking trail. And at church this morning Cindy Keen told me she got a glimpse of a naked man last night when she was walking her dog in the Meadows! She saw him between two houses on Mockingbird Lane."

"What did he do?"

"She said he tried to cover up, you know, hunched over and turned his back to her. And then he ran away into the woods. Oh, and he was wearing a shower cap on his head."

That didn't sound like any flashers I'd ever heard of. They usually ran toward people, not away, since being seen was the whole point of the exercise. The shower cap didn't make any sense at all.

I wondered if the witnesses had seen what they thought they had. It was certainly possible we had someone wandering around naked, but I wasn't convinced of it. Marta was 80 if she was a day. Maybe she'd actually seen a deer instead of a man. And if word had gotten around the neighborhood, then the power of suggestion could account for Cindy's sighting.

I thanked Tilda for the warning, then finished my ride. When I wheeled the bike into the garage fifteen minutes later I was pleased that, except for a little tenderness, my knee had handled the exercise okay.

Curtis, sprawled across the back of the sofa, opened an eye, then closed it again, when I let myself into the house. Evidently being gone for less than an hour didn't warrant a welcome.

The phone console was flashing. Linda had left a message asking me to call her as soon as possible. She answered on the first ring.

"Hey, Linda. How was the birthday party?"

"Oh, it was fine," she said. "But have you heard the news?"

"What news?"

"There were two more robberies yesterday!"

"Was your shop robbed?"

"Oh, no. Not the shop. Here in Marchpoint! The Burnetts' house was broken into and so was Dick Campbell's place."

I didn't bother to tell her that, unless someone had been home, those crimes were burglaries not robberies. We'd plowed that field too many times. "What was taken?"

She blew out an exasperated breath. "Not much, I don't think. But that's not the point! We have a crime wave going on here. We need to organize a neighborhood watch or something."

"Ummm...maybe so." I didn't think we needed a neighborhood watch. But then, I didn't think we had a problem.

"And you'd be the perfect person to organize it, Emily. I mean, with your background in..."

"Oh, no, not me. Don't even think about it."

"But..."

"If you're so big on the idea of a neighborhood watch, you do it."

"Well, maybe I will." She sounded a little huffy. "At least *I* want to do what I can to protect my neighbors from a crime wave."

I sighed. "Come on, Linda. There's no crime wave, only a few petty thefts. I'm telling you, it's probably somebody's grandkids."

"You'll see," she predicted. "We've got a real problem, Emily. You just don't want to admit it. But you'll see."

The insurance company called early Monday to let me know the Trailblazer was a complete loss.

"It's totaled, Miz Christopher. We'll be sending you a check."

Visions of a fancy new car danced in my head. However, when the cheerful young woman on the phone told me just how much my middle-aged SUV was worth, I had to rethink my plans.

I started looking that afternoon. I visited several dealerships, checking out the showroom models, and wandering around the lots. I thought I'd found what I wanted at a place near the Mall of Georgia, but a smarmy salesman changed my mind. I was examining a low-slung hatch-backed vehicle that I would have called a station wagon, but was identified as a cross-over on the label plastered to the side window, but after the salesman called me "sweetheart" seven times in fifteen minutes, I knew I was in the wrong place.

A few minutes later, I stopped at a Honda dealership. There a soft-spoken man named Edward escorted me around. He didn't try to push any one vehicle and seemed content to follow me around the lot as I looked at several. The biggest thing in his favor was that he didn't call me *dear* or *sweetie*, nor did he act as if I were too feeble to get in and out of the vehicles by myself. I'd already decided that, at the first endearment, I'd move on down the road to the Toyota dealership, but I didn't have to.

I test drove a couple of models and finally settled on a CR-V. It was spacious, had a built-in GPS, and got much better gas mileage than my old SUV. My only concern was the color.

"I was hoping for something other than gray," I told him. "Seems like every other car on the road is silver or gray."

"Oh, this isn't gray," he assured me with a straight face. "It's urban titanium. There's a big difference."

"Ummmmm."

It wasn't worth arguing over since this was the only vehicle on the lot that had every feature I wanted.

Filling out the paperwork took longer than choosing the car and it was nearly 4:00 when we finished. They promised it would be ready Wednesday afternoon.

Several of my assigned investigations still had loose ends flapping. Two I handled easily, typing and emailing the reports, but the third required a meeting with Annette Thibidoux.

Like most of what I did for the DA's office, this one involved vetting the witnesses in upcoming trials. Usually the work was routine to the point of boredom, but this case was different. Tuesday afternoon I stopped by Annette's office and laid it out for her.

"You could have a problem with the Dupree case," I told her.

She sighed. "Great. We've got this guy on seven burglaries and one attempted robbery—we go to trial next week and now you tell me there's a problem."

"Maybe, maybe not." I tried to get comfortable in the hard chair across the desk from her. "But one of your witnesses—the victim in the attempted robbery—may be a little hinky. Turns out this isn't the first time Alice Compton has been a witness in a big trial."

"Coincidences happen."

"Yeah, maybe."

Kingston Dupree had been arrested after the next-door neighbor of his seventh burglary victim spotted him carry a flat screen TV from the house to his car and drive away. She'd been quick enough to get a description of Dupree, his car and, even better, a tag number. The information was mentioned on the six o'clock news the same day. The neighbor, a very attractive young woman in a low-cut blouse, was interviewed and hailed as something of a hero for being so observant.

An hour later, Alice Compton, who lived only two blocks away from the burglary, called the police herself. She reported that a man fitting the description of the burglary suspect had broken in her back door and entered her house. She'd been laying down in her bedroom, trying to get over a headache, when she heard glass breaking. She told police she figured the man had thought the house was empty because there were no lights on.

Compton reported she'd run into the kitchen and found the man who had then moved toward her in a threatening way and demanded money. When she started screaming, he ran out the back door. She hurried to the front of the house in time to see him drive away and had been able to get a partial tag number as he passed under a street light. The partial tag matched that of the car from the earlier burglary.

The tag number came back to a Lucinda Dupree in Cobb County. Police went to the address and found her son Kingston there. A search of the car turned up the flat-screen TV and items from the other six burglaries. Kingston was arrested and charged with the burglary. He was also charged with the attempted robbery of Alice Compton. As so many burglars do, Kingston confessed not only to the latest burglary, but the six others he'd committed. Once you're caught, you might as well clean the slate. He wouldn't, however, confess to the attempted robbery.

"It's a slam-dunk case."

"But Dupree never confessed to the robbery," I said.

Annette shrugged. "Yeah, he probably knows you get more time for one robbery than a whole string of burglaries. I wouldn't confess to it either."

"Maybe so. But it's still kinda shaky—at least your victim is. When she lived in Alabama, Alice Compton reported that she'd seen a man, who had already been arrested for breaking into cars, in *her* neighborhood where some cars had been broken into. She picked him out of a photo line-up. But his picture had been shown on TV. Anyway, the guy was charged with those thefts, too, and Alice had a nice little write-up in the paper. That was ten years ago."

"Well, some people just kind of attract trouble," Annette said, sounding as if she were trying to convince herself.

"Then two years back ..."

Annette groaned.

"Two years back, when she was living down in Atlanta, the same sort of thing happened. Again, she got in the paper and, that time, she was interviewed on television, too, saying how important it was for people to get involved."

Annette was shaking her head.

"And now this," I finished. "I brought you a copy of the article where our local paper interviewed her this time. Maybe it is all co-incidence, but it could look bad in court."

"Great." She gave a big sigh. "I guess it's possible the defense won't catch it."

"Who's the attorney?"

"Your ex."

"Owen? Oh, hell. This stuff wasn't hard for me to find and he's absolutely anal about trial prep. I'll bet you lunch that he's already got it and is just waiting to use it."

She sighed again. "I guess I should say thanks, Emily. At least you've saved us from an ugly surprise. I'll talk to David about it." David Akins was one of the assistant DA's. "He may want to work out some kind of plea. Maybe even drop this count."

"Sorry I had to be the one to bring you the bad news."

She smiled and shook her head. "It's way better to know it now than to find out in front of the judge. Oh, I almost forgot," she pulled a couple of pieces of paper from her desk drawer, "I looked into Jim Lazenby. Like you said, even though he and his wife are pretty socially prominent, he's a sleaze. A whole lot of shady real estate deals, but nothing illegal as far as I can see."

'Yeah, that's my take, too."

"He does have a record of sorts, but it's not much. The charges date back to the early nineties in Athens. While he was a student there, he was arrested three times for public drunk and disorderly conduct. Paid the fines. No jail time, of course. Just another crazy college boy.

"And Franklin Eckley's death is in the record as an auto accident. As far as I could tell, there was no doubt about it. Wish I could have found more."

"Me, too," I told her. "But you can't find what's not there. There's got to be some way to stop this guy, although I don't know what it would be."

She smiled. "Well, if you figure it out and I can help, I'm ready."

SIXTEEN

AN UNUSUAL SIGHT GREETED ME WHEN I ARRIVED HOME — UNusual, at least, for Marchpoint. A Blount County patrol car sat in the driveway of a house three doors down from me. Although ambulances weren't uncommon in our community, this was the first time I'd ever seen a police car here. I pulled into the garage, then joined my next-door neighbor who was watching the goings-on from the sidewalk.

Marty Berkowitz turned as I approached. "Hey, Emily. Somebody broke into Judy's house."

"Is she okay?"

"Yeah. She's in there now with the police. She ran over to my place when she found she'd been robbed and called the cops from there."

"Did they really *break* in? I mean, kick in a door or something?"

"No, I don't believe so." He ran a hand over his nearly bald head. "I think she left her patio door unlocked."

"What was taken?"

"A coin collection, she said. Oh, and some jewelry."

"Have you been home all day?"

"Yeah." He nodded toward his open garage. "Decided it was

time to do something about that mess. I've been cleaning the place out all afternoon."

"Did you see anybody on the street?"

"Just the usual. Guy reading the water meter was here. But I know he didn't go in her backyard. I was watching him the whole time, wanted to make sure he was actually reading the meters, you know, not just writing down estimates. The Stones came by, walking that yapping dog of theirs. Oh, and that new lady who just moved into the Arbor, real pretty gal, she walked past."

"New lady?" I was afraid I knew who he meant.

"Yeah, I met her and her husband down at the clubhouse Monday. He's a lawyer, but I can't remember his name. Hers is Sarah, though. Real pretty thing, younger than him."

The bitch was back and my street was on her walking route.

"His name is Owen Christopher," I told him.

"That's right! Hey, Christopher — just like yours. That's a coincidence, isn't it?"

Milton Overton came up in his golf cart about that time. He slowed to a stop beside Marty and me, squinting at us through thick glasses. A yellow legal pad lay on the seat beside him.

"What's going on?"

"Judy Nixon had a burglary."

"Too bad." He shook his head. "We need to do something to increase security around here."

"You didn't see anything unusual today, did you?" Marty asked. If anyone would notice something out of the ordinary, it would be Milt the snitch.

"Nothing." He looked at Marty's garage door suspiciously. The covenants required all garage doors to be closed when not in use.

"I'm cleaning out the garage," Marty said quickly.

"And I just got home." Mine was open, too.

Milton gave us a nod and continued his patrolling. He wasn't one for small talk.

"He reported George Gillespie for putting the wrong color mulch in his front border," Marty said. "Poor George had to have it all removed and put the pine straw back in.

"And I heard he's proposing a new rule that folks who walk their dogs will have to carry a bottle of water with them so they can pour it on the grass where the dogs pee. It's supposed to prevent the grass from turning brown in those spots."

I just shook my head. "I keep hoping Milt will do something that violates the covenants and we can report him."

"Never happen. He's too compulsive. You should see how he separates his recyclables. I've even seen him picking up individual leaves off his lawn."

"I can still dream."

Curtis was on top of the kitchen cabinets again, but he quickly jumped down to the top of the fridge, onto the countertop and down to the floor when I came in. In seconds, he was rubbing against my legs and giving short little welcoming cries. It could have been affection, but I figured it was more likely he was ready to eat and knew I controlled the food bag.

I fed the cat, then myself, and then sat down one more time with the Coopers' papers and the stuff I'd collected on Lazenby. I still couldn't find anything useful. Lazenby had swindled the Coopers and a number of others, but he'd done it legally and well. And I thought there was a good chance he'd either killed Eckley himself or had it done, but didn't see any way to prove that either.

After a while, I put away the papers and poured myself a glass of wine. I'd had a few flickerings of ideas about how to tackle Lazenby, but nothing would gel.

About 10:00 I heard Nick come home on that noisy motorcycle. I wondered if he might call and then was annoyed with myself for hoping he would. Was I in high school again? Then the phone rang and, in spite of myself, I felt a little twinge of excitement.

"Is it true?" Linda asked breathlessly. "Was Judy Nixon robbed?"

"No," I said, unable to resist.

"But I heard she was — this afternoon."

I grinned. Sometimes I just couldn't help myself. "She wasn't *robbed*, she was *burglarized*. The two are not synonymous. If someone robs you, he steals from you face to face with force or the threat of force."

She exhaled in exasperation. "This is no time for an English lesson, Em. Did someone go in Judy's house?"

"That's what I heard."

"Oh, my God. What's happening here? I'm so scared I know I'll never be able to sleep tonight. First all these robberies and now we have a sex offender roaming the neighborhood."

It took just a second to figure out what she meant. "Have you been talking to Tilda Earle?"

"Tilda? No. But I heard that Marta Schmidt was attacked right in her own driveway!"

When we'd straightened it out and I'd convinced her that no one had been attacked — in fact, I still wasn't sure there was anything to the sightings — it was time for bed, but Linda wasn't ready to say goodnight.

For the next ten minutes, she ranted on, making it seem that a few petty thefts in Marchpoint heralded the end of civilization as we knew it. Linda would never, she declared, never feel safe in her own home again.

As much as I tried to point out that the thefts had all happened in unoccupied, unlocked houses, she wasn't reassured.

"I'll never sleep tonight! I'll just lay there waiting for someone to break in and murder me in my bed!"

"Whoa, whoa. Who said anything about murder? Linda, it's been a few small thefts and maybe some poor soul with dementia wandering around without his clothes. Let's not make more of this than we should."

"It's fine for you to talk like that," she said. "*You're* the one with a gun! If anybody breaks in on you, you can just shoot them."

"Well, not exactly…"

I heard her take a deep breath and expel it forcefully. "I know what I'm going to do. Tomorrow I'm going out and buy a gun myself!"

"Oh, I don't think that's such a great idea. Have you ever shot one before?"

"No, but it can't be that hard. I just know I'd feel safer if I had a gun."

I sighed. "Before you do that, let me take you to the range and you can shoot some and see what you think. Then if you still want a gun, I'll go with you to buy it."

She reluctantly agreed to that and we hung up. I hoped if I didn't mention it again, she'd forget about it. Linda Winkler with a gun was something no neighborhood needed.

Wednesday afternoon Linda followed me to a rental agency where I turned in the car I'd gotten in Fitzgerald, then she drove me to the Honda dealership. On the way, she still wanted to talk about Marchpoint crime.

"I just don't feel safe anymore," she said.

"Has there been another theft?"

"No, not that I've heard about. But there may be any minute."

I couldn't work up any concern. "You should be fine if you just lock your doors when you leave the house. I haven't heard of any forced entry."

"Oh, I do that, usually."

"Every time is better than usually. Any more spottings of the naked man?" I asked, hoping to lighten the mood.

"No. And I don't think I'd be upset if I saw him now. Most people seem to believe he must have Alzheimer's or something, like you said. You know, some poor old guy that just forgets to put on his clothes and wanders away."

I was relieved to hear that sanity might be making a comeback.

My new ride was waiting right out in front at the dealership. Freshly washed, it sat in the parking lot, gleaming in the autumn sunlight. And Edward had been right. It wasn't just gray. In this light it shone a combination of bronze and silver. Urban titanium, it was.

"It's so cute!" Linda said.

I hadn't been aiming for cute, just utilitarian. But I had to admit the car had a certain panache. More compact than my old SUV, it looked modern and frisky. And the fact that it should almost double the miles per gallon I was used to getting didn't hurt either.

Linda left me there and, after signing a few more papers, I

climbed into the CR-V and drove off the lot. I've never been one to rhapsodize about new car smell or the glories of any machine, but I admit I did enjoy the drive home.

I spent Thursday and Friday in a hallway in the Superior Court building with fifteen other witnesses—unprofitable time for me. I bill by the case, not the hour. Unlike the several police officers I shared a bench with, I wasn't paid to sit there.

My name was on the DA's list as a "just in case" witness, there in the unlikely event that something came up about the other witnesses that I'd vetted. As usual, I wasn't called to testify. The only good thing about the experience was that I caught up on my reading.

All week, the stores, radio, and television had been full of Thanksgiving and I was beginning to dread spending the holiday alone. So Friday night, I called my daughter Chelsea in South Carolina and took her up on her standing invitation.

"Oh, I'm so glad you're coming, Mom. It's going to be a great dinner! I found a fantastic new recipe for apple and chestnut soup, and I'm making my pumpkin chiffon pie that everybody loves. Oh, and Pier One had the cutest place card holders—they're the sweetest little turkeys, autumn colors and lots of glitter!"

Chelsea made Martha Stewart look like an amateur. I don't know where she got it —certainly not from me. And I didn't see that we needed place cards—it would only be family around the table and we all knew each other pretty well, but I put enthusiasm in my voice and said, "It sounds just wonderful, darling."

She invited me to drive up Wednesday afternoon and stay over until Friday. "I've just redone the guest room, all in mauve and violet. You'll love it."

"I'm sure I will, but I can't stay until Friday." I knew two nights in house beautiful would be a strain. I'm something of a social and fashion disappointment to my daughter and she wouldn't be able to resist trying to help me improve in those areas for more than 24 hours. Then I realized I had a built-in excuse. "I can't leave the cat alone for that long."

"You got a cat? I'm so glad! It'll give you some company, living alone like you do. Why don't you bring the cat with you? The kids would love it."

"No, that's not a good idea. He...he doesn't travel well."

Saturday was the day I reserved for cleaning house. I finished my chores by 2:00 and was idly flipping through the TV channels when Nick Buckley called and invited me to dinner.

"I'd like that. What time do you want to leave?"

"We're not going anywhere. All you have to do is walk to my house and I'll take it from there."

He cooked? I was surprised. Owen never did anything more than pour cereal and milk into a bowl. Of course, he always had someone—me and now Sarah—to do the cooking for him.

"So how about it? You want to come over here about 7:00?"

The idea of an evening alone with Nick was vaguely dangerous. I almost refused, but agreed instead and at 7:00 on the dot I was ringing his bell.

SEVENTEEN

THE FIRST THING I NOTICED WAS NICK — LOOKING FIT AND disturbingly sexy in jeans and a blue oxford cloth shirt. The second was the music softly filling the air. A woman vowing to walk from Boulder to Birmingham.

I smiled. "Emmylou. Nice."

He looked pleasantly surprised. "You like Emmylou Harris?"

"Love her. Been a fan for years."

"Me, too. You can always count on Emmylou. She can get you through just about anything."

He led me to the living room where everything was neat and no packing boxes remained. I accepted a glass of wine, just to be nice, and took a sip. I was surprised that it wasn't too bad.

When I was settled on the sofa, he asked, "Is there anything new with that mess down south? The guy who tried to kill you?"

"Jim Lazenby. No, I haven't come up with anything I can use against him."

"He has to be vulnerable somewhere. Didn't you tell us he wanted to run for office?"

"Yeah, but I don't think that's going to do us any good. I practically threatened to go public with his business practices, but it's not enough. Of course, it must have bothered him some." I grinned. "He did have me run off the road."

He sipped his wine. "Don't suppose there's any way to prove that."

"Nothing I can think of. I couldn't ID the driver even if they found him." I shrugged. "And Lazenby just keeps on, knowing nobody is going to stop him."

A slow smile crossed Nick's face. "He may have just met his match."

"Me?" I laughed. "I'd like to think so, but right now I don't have a clue as to how to take him down. I'm afraid he'll keep on keeping on, get elected, and have a wonderful life."

"Yeah. What is that old saying, the only thing that could keep him from getting elected is being found in bed with a dead girl or a live boy."

"Just about. Although today the live boy might not be that much of a problem."

Dinner was pasta with shrimp and a nice light cream sauce. The music had progressed to Son Volt, then Steve Earle, and the volume was low enough that it made a nice background while we got to know each other.

LIke me, Nick was divorced, but his split had happened over twenty years before and there was no bitterness in his voice when he talked about it. He had two sons. The older, Ronald, worked with him in the family business. The younger, Adam, was a high school teacher.

"I'm surprised you haven't remarried after all this time."

He laughed. "Yeah, somehow I've been able to resist. Was it Oscar Wilde that said a second marriage was the triumph of hope over experience? Well, I've never been that hopeful. What about you?"

"Never again," I vowed. "Once was enough for me."

We returned to the living room with another glass of wine. I was actually starting to like the stuff. Maybe I'd been too hasty years ago when I decided I hated it. This time Nick sat beside me on the sofa and I was surprised at the little surge of excitement — or fear? —that shot through me.

The music changed again — he must have had it programed to shuffle artists and songs — and Nancy Griffith was replaced by a song about abandonment and travel. Nick saw that I'd noticed the change.

"You know this guy?"

I smiled. "Robert Earl Keen. That's his latest, I think. *I Gotta Go*."

He shook his head. "How do you *know* that?"

"You know it. Why shouldn't I?"

"You just don't seem like the type."

"Just what type am I?" I asked with a smile.

"Well, let's see. You're health conscious — the bike riding and the way you watch your portions. You're very structured. I'll bet you have lists for everything from grocery shopping to social obligations. Not surprising when you consider what you do for a living. And you're impatient."

"Why do you say that?"

He laughed. "When you're going to the mailbox, you raise your garage door. But you never can wait until it's all the way up. You always duck out while it's still moving."

"Have you been *watching* me?"

He smiled. "Not intentionally, but I can't help noticing things."

"So how do all your observations lead you to the conclusion that I wouldn't know Robert Earl Keen?"

He shrugged. "He just seems a little too laid back for you."

I turned to face him on the sofa. "You really don't have a clue about who I am, do you?"

He got a funny look in his eye and said slowly, "No, but I'm going to. Sooner or later, I think I'm going to know you very well."

And he kissed me. While the sweet kiss he'd given me leaving my house a week ago had been friendly, this one was downright carnal. He kissed me in a way I hadn't been kissed in years. He wrapped his arms around me and pulled me to him so that I was facing him, half in his lap.

After a few enjoyable minutes of that, we pulled apart to catch our breaths.

"Goodness," I managed to say.

"That's something of an understatement."

He moved toward me again, but I pulled back and started disentangling myself.

"I think I'd better go home before this gets totally out of control," I said. I struggled to my feet, a little embarrassed. I was acting like a high school girl making out on the sofa.

"That's just what I was hoping would happen." He was a bit breathless as well. "I'd like to see you out of control."

"Uh...some other time, maybe." Why did I say *that*? "It was a lovely dinner—a very nice evening. Thank you for inviting me."

"We have to do this again real soon," he said. "But it'll have to wait a little while. I'm leaving town tomorrow night."

"Portugal?"

"Yeah. I'll be gone about ten days."

I wished him a safe trip and slipped out. During the walk back to my house, I had to fight an urge to turn around and go back, but I successfully resisted. What in the world was wrong with me?

Sunday and Monday were slow, but things got lively—in a scary sort of way—Tuesday morning. The bell rang before 9:00. I damn near dropped my coffee cup when I opened the door to find Linda Winkler holding a gun.

"Look what I got!" In her paisley and lace, she looked like a child with a new toy. "Isn't it cute?" She turned the little revolver this way and that, admiring it. "It's just my size, not like some of those huge, ugly things they had in the display case."

She slipped past me into the house. I followed, hoping she wouldn't shoot me before I could get the thing away from her. "Where did you *get* that?"

"At the gun store up near the outlet mall." She was waving it around again. For a micro second I was looking right down the barrel.

"Be careful with that!"

She dropped onto the sofa. "It's not loaded, Emily! They wouldn't sell me a loaded gun. I had to buy the bullets separately. Did you know you have to buy a *whole box*? They won't sell you just a few bullets."

"Yes, I did know that. Ummm...may I see it?" I asked gently. I didn't want to do anything to cause more of that waving around.

"Sure."

I plucked it carefully from her fingers, popped the cylinder out and made sure it was unloaded. "The first thing you should know about a gun is that you *always* treat it like it's loaded. Always." I tested the weight of the little revolver. It fit neatly into my hand. It was a blue steel Luger LCR-22. "It's a handy little piece. Have you shot it yet?"

"No, you said you'd teach me."

I took a deep breath. "And I will. The sooner the better if you're going to be carrying it around."

An hour later, we were standing in a booth at Logan's Firing Range. At 10:00 in the morning we were the only customers. I'd brought along my Taurus Ultra-Lite, figuring I might as well get in some practice, too. We bought target rounds for both weapons and a couple of targets.

Linda was practically vibrating with excitement as I explained the range rules. "You never point that pistol anywhere but down range. When you finish shooting, put it on the bench in front of you."

"Okay, okay, I understand," she said impatiently. "I'll be careful. When do we shoot?"

I attached a paper target to the track and sent it down range about four yards. Then I made sure she had her eye and ear protection properly positioned and we were off.

It wasn't what Linda was expecting. She gave a little "ohh" of surprise when she fired the first shot. The recoil pushed her hand and the gun several inches up in the air. She emptied her gun, put it down and stepped back.

"I never even hit the target!" she complained.

I stepped around her and fired my five shots. Not a great grouping, but they were all center mass. I showed her how to eject the brass cartridges from her pistol and did the same with the .38.

"We just throw them on the floor?" she asked.

"We'll pick them up later."

"I didn't think it would be this hard," she said as we reloaded. "How does anyone ever manage to hit the bulls-eye? Or even get close to it?"

"Practice," I told her. "Practice, practice, practice until it just becomes automatic."

"Oh."

We shot for another forty minutes, but Linda's heart wasn't in it. She'd seen too many movies and expected it to be an easy, point-and-shoot experience. She was disappointed and I could tell the novelty of having a firearm was nearly gone.

We picked up our brass and put it in the bucket. Then, in the area set aside for it, I showed her how to clean a gun. She did it, but wrinkled her nose at the smell and the mess left behind.

"So, are you going to carry that thing with you?" I asked. "Because if you are, you'll need a carry permit."

She shook her head. "I don't think so. Maybe I'll just keep it in a drawer."

"You might want to keep the bullets in another place — somewhere hard to get to. Your grandkids are at your house all the time. You don't want them to get hold of that gun."

She sighed. "Yeah, I'll take care of it."

Reality is a sobering thing. I was pretty sure Linda's interest in owning a gun was over.

EIGHTEEN

BY 3:30 WEDNESDAY AFTERNOON I WAS ON THE ROAD. THE holiday traffic was so bad that it was after 7:00 when I pulled into the drive at Chelsea's house in Greenville.

The house was immaculate, as always, and my mother was already ensconced in the big recliner in the family room. Marla Miller Appling knew she was a queen and expected to be treated as such. My dad had convinced her of that fact when they'd first married and had spoiled her rotten until he passed away back in the early 90s.

Don't misunderstand. Mother had always taken good care of my dad, brother, and me. There was never any doubt that she loved us with all her heart. But we also knew that she needed a certain amount of coddling.

She now resided in an independent living home in Greenville where the staff, I was sure, continued to see to her every need. I drove up to visit her every couple of weeks, but Chelsea had become her go-to person for everyday wants and whims. From what I could tell, my daughter took the situation in stride, applying all her high-end home-making skills to her grandmother's home just as she did to her own. My son-in-law Hal was always available to rearrange furniture whenever Mother felt it needed to be done, usually a couple of times a month.

Mother's apartment was beautifully decorated and she never lacked for new clothes. I didn't bring her clothes anymore because she never liked what I chose. Her taste and Chelsea's were perfectly aligned, but they both had serious misgivings about mine.

That evening, Mother wore a black turtleneck top, trousers, and a deep green velour blazer. Diamonds sparkled at her neck and in her ears. Chelsea was equally well turned out in a fitted, cowl-collared red jersey dress and heels so high they made my feet hurt just looking at them. I brought the fashion level down a few notches. My jeans were old and comfortable and my sweatshirt had Blount County Police emblazoned across the front. Fortunately, the still-healing scratches on my face and neck were enough of a distraction for both of them that my own outfit only provoked a single comment from Mother.

"Jeans? Surely jeans are more appropriate for younger people, Emily."

But Chelsea didn't even notice. "Oh, my God, Mom, what happened to your face?"

"I was in an accident. Nothing serious, although I did total the car."

She frowned. "Was it your fault?" I could see her wondering if she was going to have to have the 'it's time to take away the keys' talk with me.

"No, Chelsea. It was not my fault."

Before she could ask any more questions, my ten-year-old grandson looked up from whatever video game he was playing. "You got a new car, Grandma? What did you get?"

"Come on, Isaac, I'll show you."

We adjourned to the driveway so everyone could admire the

CR-V and the subjects of my accident and my jeans were laid to rest. Even Mother didn't mention them again, although she did manage to get in a dig or two about my leaving Owen.

All along it had been her opinion that I should have stayed with the cheating lout because that's what a lady did. A lady preserved the family at all costs. That was only one of the numerous tenets that she'd pounded into my head all my life. A few of the others were that a lady only eats or drinks while sitting down, a lady never makes others feel uncomfortable and, my favorite, a lady never leaves the house without makeup because she owes it to other people to look her best at all times. Is it any wonder I rebelled?

My family was genuinely concerned that I'd been hurt and, when Chelsea learned I'd also twisted my knee, she declared I wasn't to lift a finger while I was there. So for a couple of days, there were two queens in the household and I didn't mind a bit.

I was absolutely cosseted that night and the next day. Isaac and his sister Cordelia behaved like angels and Chelsea and Hal saw that I had everything I needed. When I left Greenville Thursday afternoon, I was glowing with family love and stuffed to the gills with Thanksgiving dinner.

It was while I was driving home that I got the first inkling of an idea about tackling the Coopers' problem. I didn't try to force it, just let it simmer in the back of my mind.

Curtis and I had a pleasant reunion. It was good to be home, even after just one night away, and when I woke the next morning, my idea about dealing with Lazenby had coalesced into a vague sort of plan.

About 9:00 I called Annette Thibidoux. There was no answer at her house and I belatedly remembered that it was Black Friday, a world class shopping day, and Annette was nothing if not a world class shopper. Calling her cell would be a waste of time. It was nearly 6:00 that night before I got in touch with her.

"Let's meet for lunch tomorrow. I think you should explore the possibility of becoming a psychic."

"Sure," she said, "just what I've always wanted to do. It's right up there with survivalist and astronaut. But I can't do it tomorrow. There're a boatload of sales I missed today. I'll be at the Mall of Georgia by eight in the morning. This time tomorrow I'll be done with every bit of my Christmas shopping."

Listening to her made me feel tired. "I wouldn't dream of tearing you away from something that important. Do you think you'll be all shopped out by Sunday? Come over that afternoon."

"Falcons game?" She liked football almost as much as I did.

"Sure. I'll give you supper, too."

"Okay. You going to tell me what this is about?"

"No. I think I'll let it be a surprise."

Sunday was cloudy, windy and almost cold, a perfect day to stay inside. My knee was just about back to normal and I no longer looked a victim when I glanced in a mirror.

I made a pot of chili and a pan of cornbread, so Annette and I ate well as we watched the Falcons pull one out in the last quarter and beat Carolina. Then it was time to get down to business.

"Jim Lazenby is a bad man," I told her. "He's a cheat and a thief and he tried to have me killed. Somebody has to stop him."

Annette nodded her agreement. She's a good listener. It's one of the things that makes her such an effective investigator. She sat silently, wine glass balanced between long fingers, while I talked. I told her about Lazenby's wife and about Miss Gene.

"What I've got in mind isn't exactly illegal, at least most of it isn't," I said, "but if you pushed it to the extreme, it *might* be considered theft by deception. And it just might be dangerous. So if you don't want to be a part of this, I'll understand."

She smiled. "How can I refuse such an attractive offer?" The smile disappeared. "He tried to *kill* you, Emily. I think I'll hang around for this one, on one condition."

"Anything."

"I get to meet Miss Gene. I've never met a real live witch before."

"I'm sure that can be arranged. After all, you're going to be colleagues."

"Just what do you want me to do?"

"Dress exotically, look beautiful, be clairvoyant, and get Robin Lazenby to give you $8,000. No, let's make it $10,000. Her husband ought to cover our expenses and the deductible on my insurance."

Annette, the most serene person I know, didn't even blink. After a moment, she nodded slowly and said, "Only problem I see is that I don't know a thing about being clairvoyant. Think there's an accelerated class I could take?"

I laughed. "Well, maybe you don't have to be psychic—just read tarot cards or a crystal ball. And I think I know someone who might help there."

She smiled. "Linda, of course. You know she'll want to do it herself."

"I know." I shook my head, "But she's way too innocent to be involved in something like this."

Annette grinned. "Thanks a lot."

"Oh, you know what I mean. I don't think she knows how to lie and I doubt she'd be any good at getting money out of Robin Lazenby. Linda'd be more likely to tell her that her aura was ragged and she needed to delve into her intuitive side. Then she'd show her some yoga postures and volunteer to walk the dog. No, Linda can't do this."

Annette refilled her wine glass, took a small sip, then said, "I still don't understand how you think I'm going to get $10,000 out of this woman. She doesn't know me from Adam's house cat. And even if she's a flake, she's not completely stupid, is she? Why would she hand over money like that?"

"Because you're going to tell her there's a curse on it."

She laughed out loud. "That's crazy!"

"It is," I agreed. "But it's been working pretty well for hundreds of years. It's an old gypsy swindle."

"Guess I don't know any old gypsies, 'cause I've never heard of it."

"Actually, I think the term gypsy is politically incorrect these days. The proper term is Romani. And I learned about the scams when I was working with the PD. We hardly see any in the DA's office because the thefts are usually fairly small and a lot of people are too embarrassed to report it. But it still goes on.

"There are hundreds of variations, I guess, but very simply a fortune teller declares that her victim—or in this case her victim's husband—is cursed, usually because of some terrible thing they've done in the past. The curse can be on anything of value—gold, silver, paper money, jewelry, whatever. And the only way to get rid of the curse is to get rid of the items."

"No. Uhn uhhh. I tell her the money is cursed and she gives

it to me and walks away? That is *not* going to happen. Nobody is dumb enough to fall for that."

"But they are. Oh, it's not done cold. The con artist usually takes weeks to gain the trust of the victim."

"Sounds like a lot more time than we've got to give."

"Yeah, we'll have to accelerate the process, I know. But I think it can be done."

"If you say so." She didn't sound convinced.

I stepped into the kitchen to get another beer and a paperback. "Here," I said, handing her the book. "I fought the crazy holiday shoppers yesterday and found this at Barnes & Noble."

She raised an eyebrow. "Not exactly on the New York Times bestseller list, I'd guess?"

I nodded at the garish cover. "I know it looks corny, but it's got some good information. Describes how fortunetellers scam their victims. How they build trust."

She shook her head. "My mother would never approve of her child learning how to cheat people." She laughed. "But she's in Memphis and won't ever know about it, I guess. And it's for a good cause."

We talked for another hour. When Annette left, I thought we'd covered every contingent. I certainly hoped so.

NINETEEN

ANNETTE THIBIDOUX'S LOFT IN DOWNTOWN MARINVILLE, was a reflection of herself—cool, elegant, and completely controlled. Long gray leather sofas and low ebony tables made an inviting conversational nook. There were no knickknacks. Only a book and two magazines disturbed the surface of the furniture. The kitchen was neat, utilitarian, and equipped the way it should be for a woman who enjoyed cooking and only settled for the best. The dining table nearby was bare except for a muted blue pottery bowl in the center. Her bedroom area was hidden behind large, sliding Japanese shoji screens.

The only uncontrolled elements in the place were the two white standard poodles and a lanky man lounging on one of the sofas.

"Hey," she said. "I thought you were still in Atlanta."

"Got back early." Scott Barksdale got up, crossed to where she stood and planted a lingering kiss on her lips. "I missed you."

She grinned up into his eyes. "Missed you, too." She rubbed a hand up his arm, the wool soft under her fingers. "And you're looking really fine tonight."

"You're just saying that because you're a lonely, single career woman who's hungry for companionship."

She laughed. "What an insightful man."

"Where have you been?"

"Oh, I went to Emily's. We watched the game."

A minute passed. "When am I going to meet her? Or any of your other friends?"

Annette sighed. She really didn't want to get into this right now. "Sometime soon."

"You've been saying that for three months."

"We've talked about this, Scott. You know how I feel about you, but the two of us out in public ..."

"Public? You act like it's the 1950s. You and I aren't really big news anymore. Interracial couples hardly raise an eyebrow these days. In fact, I don't think any kind of couples do. Besides, we're talking about your friend's house, you know?"

The dogs nudged between them, a welcome distraction. Annette leaned over to scratch two curly heads. "I see you, guys. Do you need a walk?"

"They do not," Scott said. "They've been walked and fed and walked again. But they'd be much happier in a house with a nice big yard, don't you think?"

"A big house like yours?"

"Well, yeah. For example."

She put her arms around his neck and kissed him again. "Let's not fuss about that tonight, hon. I'm beat and I have to learn how to be a gypsy."

She poured herself a glass of the wine he'd already opened and related what she and Emily had discussed.

"And you're actually going to go to this godforsaken place in south Georgia and commit fraud because ...?"

"This couple really needs help. The guy swindled them out of everything they had. And he damn near killed Emily. He needs to pay."

"And you and Emily are the ones to make him?"

"Yeah, we are."

"You need to think about this, Annette. If you end up getting arrested, you'll lose everything you have."

She felt bad because she could see how worried he was. "It's not going to come to that. And you did hear me, didn't you? He tried to *kill* Emily."

He gave up with a sigh and pulled her to him. "Okay, okay. You're a grown woman and can do what you want. And may I say, you're very nicely grown."

Scott left before ten, pleading an early meeting, but Annette thought he might just be making the point that, if she didn't want him full time, she'd better learn to get along without him.

A familiar heaviness in her chest sent her to the medicine cabinet and one of the small white pills her doctor had prescribed the previous week, along with the advice to avoid stress. Fat chance that was going to happen. She'd probably end up in the hospital one of these days.

After a brisk walk up Sycamore Street, Annette felt better and the dogs were calmer and happy to curl up beside her on the sofa while she read the book Emily had given her. She gave it her full attention, as she did every other thing in her life that mattered. She took notes from time to time on a yellow legal pad and occasionally shook her head at the gullibility of people who'd fall for such crazy things. At one point, she laughed out loud and reached for her phone.

TWENTY

ANNETTE HAD LEFT EARLY AND, BY ELEVEN, CURTIS AND I were in bed. I was reading and he was catching up on much needed sleep.

The phone rang.

"I'll tell you one thing right now," Annette said. "I'm not breaking open a blood-filled egg for any—damn—body."

"What are you talking about?"

"It's right here in this book you gave me. Listen to this shit: 'After being told during her previous visit to the fortune teller that her family was cursed, Mary Ellen was instructed to return the following week and bring an egg from her own refrigerator. When she arrived back at the fortune teller's house, the woman took the egg from her. In the darkened room, the fortune teller performed a sleight of hand trick and substituted an egg she had prepared in advance. Then, before her victim's horrified eyes, she broke the egg into a glass bowl and what looked like blood gushed out. The fortune teller advised that this meant the curse was much worse than she had thought.' Yuck! I'm not doing that!"

I laughed. "I don't think we'll have to go that far."

"You better hope we don't or you'll lose your tame fortune teller before I even get started." She sobered. "Just when are you thinking about pulling off this charade?"

"Thursday and Friday."

"What Thursday and Friday?"

"This week."

"Are you out of your mind? That's three days from now."

"Yeah, but we need to do it soon. I think we should get in and out fast, before we give them too much time to think. You'll be able to get off work, won't you?"

"Oh, sure. There aren't any trials for my unit this week and I've got more leave built up than anybody in the office. They're always after me to take time off." She sighed. "Thursday and Friday, hmmmm? I guess I better get Linda to teach me what she can. Give me her phone number and I'll see what we can set up."

TWENTY-ONE

THE DOGS, JULES AND JACQUES, GREETED ANNETTE FRANTI- cally when she got out of bed Monday morning. It was nearly eight and they were more than ready for a walk.

"I know, I know," she said, hooking them up to their leashes. "I slept late, didn't I?"

They almost dragged her into the elevator. They rushed out of the building to the small park across the street. While the dogs took care of their needs, Annette called the office and talked with her boss. Even with no prior notice, McDaniel was happy to give her the week off.

"I hope you'll relax and have some fun," he told her.

"I'll try."

Linda arrived at her door early that afternoon in a swirl of peasant skirt, gauzy blouse, and fringed paisley shawl. Her gray and blond hair hung shiny and straight to the middle of her back. She carried a battered denim back pack in one hand and greeted Annette with a big smile.

Annette ushered her in. "I really appreciate you helping out like this."

"Oh, no problem. I'm glad to—wow! What a cool place!" It

was Linda's first time in the loft. While she and Annette knew each other, their contact was a product of their friendship with Emily.

"Thanks. I like it."

Linda spent a few minutes on the floor, getting to know the dogs, then remembered why she was there, got to her feet, and motioned to the table in the dining nook.

"Can we use that?"

"Sure. Would you like some coffee or something?"

"No, thanks." Linda was unloading an assortment of curious items from her bag and placing them on the tabletop. "Just had lunch, so I'm good."

Before they began, Linda wanted to clear the air. "Look, I know you and Emily don't believe in the psychic world. Let me tell you, Emily made that clear forty years ago! I'm okay with that, even though I'm not really comfortable with y'all pretending to do this thing in Fitzgerald.

"I mean, it's *real*, you know? You may not think so, but it is. And this is almost like I'm helping you make fun of something I believe in." She took a deep breath. "But I know it's for a good cause and all. So, I guess we'd better get to it."

Annette had had some lessons over the years. Some good — like being taught to make a demi-glace by a really good chef — and some bad — like being tasered as part of her police training — but this was the strangest one ever.

"Now this is a crystal ball," Linda explained unnecessarily. She took the glass orb from its cloth wrapping and set it on a little ebony stand. "Personally, I can't do much with one of these things. My grandmama could, but all I ever see is reflections of what's right around me in the room." She moved it nearer to Annette's chair. "But you never know. Why don't you give it a try?"

Annette obediently stared into the ball. She didn't even see reflections. All she saw was glass.

"Listen, Linda," she began apologetically, "I don't really expect to be able to see the future. You know that, don't you? I just have to be convincing enough to fool somebody into thinking that I can."

"Oh, I know. But I wouldn't want you to miss an opportunity. I mean, I've always known I've had the sight—well, since I was three and told Mama that Mrs. Huckabee down the road had passed over before anyone knew it—but it can come to folks at different times in their lives. So it's worth trying."

"Okay," Annette said. Although she thought she was more likely to have a meteor crash through the roof of her loft than to suddenly develop psychic powers, if such things even existed, which she was pretty sure they didn't. "Well, I don't see anything in the crystal ball."

Linda nodded. "All right. Let's try the cards."

Over the next hour, Linda tried to give Annette an overview of the tarot. "The cards are really just a means to focus your concentration. And if you just look at them and go with your feelings, they'll lead you to the truth. The major arcana—these with names instead of suits—are almost self-explanatory. See?"

"Ummm ... I really don't."

"Just look at the pictures. Like this one." She held up a card showing a vaguely medieval drawing of a lightning-struck tower with hapless victims falling from its heights. "This is called the tower of destruction."

"That makes sense, I guess."

"But it doesn't mean you're going to be struck by lightning. It represents unexpected events. It can mean catastrophe, upset, violent change." She held up another card—this showed a skeleton astride a fierce-looking, white horse. The word DEATH was written across the bottom.

"That's pretty easy to understand, I guess. Don't you have any cheerful cards in that deck?"

"Just wait. This is the death card, yes. But it doesn't always mean death in the literal sense of the word. It often signals dramatic change, leaving one life and moving into another."

"To me, that's not ever going to mean anything but death."

Linda smiled. "I know. Lots of people react that way. When this card shows up in a reading, I have to calm 'em down and explain it doesn't have to mean death." Her smile disappeared. "Of course, sometimes that's exactly what it does mean."

Annette was becoming interested in spite of herself. "So what do you do then? I mean, do you just tell somebody they're going to *die*?"

"No, of course not. I'd never do that to someone. But I might tell them they need to take better care of themselves—especially if the rest of the reading indicates medical problems—and suggest they see a doctor."

Annette didn't feel a single thing looking at all the cards except confusion. "Do you really *see* things, Linda?"

"Well, it's more like I *know* them. I mean, I don't actually see the picture of what I'm feeling, but I know what's going to happen."

Linda pulled a diagram she'd drawn from her backpack and then flipped through the deck to find the cards she thought were just right for Robin Lazenby's reading.

"I've numbered the spaces on the diagram in the order the cards should be placed," Linda said. "And on the back, there's a list of each card, the corresponding number in the diagram, and what you will need to tell her about each one." She gave Annette a critical look. "It will take some practice to do this right."

"I don't mind putting in some work, but I can't see how I'm going to be able to get those cards in those spots when I do a reading for her." Annette frowned. "I mean, she may be a little nuts, but she's not stupid. She'll expect me to shuffle the deck, won't she?"

Linda nodded. "I've thought about that and...uh...I think I've got a way you can do it. Tarot cards are traditionally wrapped in a silk cloth." She reached in the backpack and pulled out a bright, paisley scarf. "I thought this would work.

"What you need to do is take those cards," she indicated the diagram, "and keep them in the right order in a separate stack." She scooped up the ones she'd laid out and placed them next to the rest of the deck. "See, you can keep the ones you want to use divided from the rest by a layer of cloth. Then, when you first unwrap the deck, keep the selected cards back and put the rest of the deck on the table." She demonstrated. "Then kind of pile the scarf on top of the ones you held back and slip it into your lap."

She showed how that could be accomplished while Annette watched, her lips pursed in doubt.

"I don't know that I can do that."

"Well, you'll need to practice, of course. And it's a good idea to distract her while you're doing it. Ask a question about something in the store or make an observation, so that she'll look at something else.

"Then shuffle the rest of the deck in front of her. When you're ready, lay the deck down, pick up the scarf with the other cards, like you're gathering the fabric up in both hands and lay the silk over the deck. That way you can put the extra cards right on top."

She demonstrated the move. "Then you want to distract her while you're lining the cards up, so you might rub your hands all over them and say something like, you want their energy to help with the reading. Oh, I don't know, but say something and you can manipulate the cards under the silk.

"Then, carefully remove the scarf," she said, showing Annette how to do it, "and you're ready for the reading."

Annette looked at the cards, then at Linda. "It's hard for me to believe you just thought about how to do that and then did it. I don't mean to be insulting, but it looks to me like you've had some practice in stacking that tarot deck."

Linda dropped her eyes to the table and her face turned pink. Emily was right. Linda Winkler couldn't lie to save her soul.

"Well ... yes ... I've actually done it a couple of times — but only for a good cause." She took a deep breath. "Once when my daughter Andrea decided she wanted to drop out of college and become a tattoo artist. And then, when Jeremy thought he was in love with that hateful little girl from Tucson..." She shook her head. "I know it was wrong, but I felt like I had to do something really dramatic, so they'd see what was right." She took another breath and pushed it out hard. "I think God will forgive me for misusing my talent in those situations — and in this one."

Annette reached across the table and patted the other woman's hand. "I'm sure He will."

Before she left, Linda insisted on doing a reading for her.

"Oh, that's not necessary, really."

But Linda was adamant. "You need to see how it's done. And I wouldn't feel right sending you off on something like this without making sure everything was going to be all right."

So Annette sat quietly as Linda proceeded to lay out ten cards in the same pattern she'd used for Robin Lazenby's cards. She called it the Celtic cross.

There were confusing bright colors and pictures that meant nothing to Annette. However, one card was immediately recognizable. A skeleton in black armor, riding a white horse.

Linda was silent as she looked at the cards spread on the table before her. She exhaled hard. "Well ... it's not the best spread."

"What's wrong with it?" Annette asked and then felt like an idiot for asking. It was just a bunch of cards, death card or not.

"Ummm ... parts of it aren't too bad. I mean, Justice is what's driving you in this enterprise." She indicated a card where a woman sat on a throne with a stern look on her face and an upright sword in her right hand."

"Yeah, well, that's good, isn't it?" Annette asked. "And these two people holding goblets look pretty happy."

"That's your recent past. The two of cups signifies romance. A happy couple."

A picture of Scott flashed in Annette's mind and she realized why fortune telling worked. The subject, or victim, as she saw it, was primed and ready to take whatever the reader said and find a way to apply it to her own life.

"And this one, the six of pentacles, is your near future. It indicates you'll be in a position to help someone financially," Linda went on.

Annette wondered what the hell a pentacle was, but didn't ask.

"But it's the outcome cards here that worry me," Linda said. "The ten of cups reversed *could* just mean the disruption of a happy relationship—like breaking up with a boyfriend. But it can also represent loss and sadness. There's the eight of wands reversed. That's fraud and cheating and dishonesty. And, of course, the Death card."

Annette refused to buy into all of this. "Yeah, but you said it just meant change."

"Ummhmmm, it can. But it's the outcome card in this spread. It means significant change, upsetting change, a figurative death of your old life and rebirth. But ..." She looked straight into Annette's eyes and held the gaze for a minute. "But it can also mean real death, especially in a negative spread."

"We're going to be fine," Annette said, trying to get away from this subject. She'd had about all the metaphysical nonsense she could take for one day. "I just have to learn to be a magician in a couple of days."

As Linda repacked her bag, she tried to dissuade Annette from going ahead with the plan. "Look, I know you don't believe in it. But I'm telling you — I saw it in the cards and you don't need to go to that town. It's dangerous for you and Emily both, but especially for you. Something bad could happen, Annette. Please don't go."

Annette eased the worried woman out of the apartment, promising they'd be extra careful. "From what Emily says, it'll all be over this time next week."

At the door, Linda gave her a spontaneous hug. "I'll pray for you."

Then she was gone.

Annette went back inside to practice the tarot. She felt like she was cramming for a final.

TWENTY-TWO

I KEPT GOING OVER THE PLAN IN MY HEAD. THERE WAS NO guarantee it would work, but I wanted to try, particularly since it was absolutely the only thing I'd been able to come up with. Lazenby needed to pay for what he'd done to the Coopers and to me, and who knew how many others.

The weather continued cool and rainy and on Tuesday I decided a swim might be a better choice than a bike ride. Marchpoint's crowning glory was the amenities center, located in the center of the subdivision. It boasted a ballroom, a craft studio, a huge gym, and an enormous indoor pool. I hurriedly changed in the locker room and made my way there.

Only a couple of people were in the big, window-lined enclosure. One man that I didn't recognize swam laps. A woman whose name I thought was Becky... how could anyone be expected to remember the names of all the people in this huge community? ... relaxed in the jacuzzi. I stepped down into the pool, pleased it wasn't too warm, and started my own laps.

I gave up trying to keep count of my laps long ago, instead keeping an eye on the clock on the interior wall. When I'd been at it for 30 minutes, I stopped and made my slow way out of the pool. Swimming always left me feeling limp and worn out, but it was a good feeling none the less. I toweled the water from my hair, patted down my body as well as I could and started back to the locker room.

"Well, hello, Emily." There was no greeting in that voice. It dripped with loathing.

I turned to face Sarah Candler Christopher, my former friend and Owen's current wife. As so often seemed to happen, I was at a disadvantage in the encounter—dripping wet, hair plastered to my head, my less than perfect figure displayed in an old, clinging suit. Sarah, on the other hand, looked like one of those actresses about whom people always said, 'I can't believe she could be in her forties'. Her hair was beautifully coiffed, golden and curling around her perfectly made up face. Even though I knew she'd had a tiny bit of help from a surgeon, I couldn't find fault with the finished product. She was lovely. And the body she worked so hard to maintain was attractively displayed in bright, new workout clothes.

"Hello, Sarah. I heard you and Owen moved in here."

"Yes, we're settling in nicely." She looked around to be sure we weren't overheard. Sarah was nothing if not circumspect. "I'd hoped we could just get along here, but that was before you started spreading rumors about me."

Well, that was completely unexpected. "What the hell are you talking about?"

"Evidently you think I'm a thief. The *police* came and talked to me last week just because I was walking on your street."

"I never talked to the police and I wouldn't have said anything about you if I had." But Marty Berkowitz must have since he was the only person I'd mentioned Sarah's name to. Right then, I knew I could have turned on the sweetness, smoothed everything over and we'd both have gone our way, but I couldn't resist stirring things up a bit. "However, it does seem strange that you've been right there when some of the burglaries have occurred. Several people have mentioned it."

Her lower lip quivered a bit. "Oh, how could you be so mean? We used to be friends, Emily."

"That was before you screwed my husband in my own bed. I believe that's grounds for discontinuing our friendship." I wrapped the towel around my shoulders with as much dignity as I could. "As far as the thefts go, I'll repeat that I didn't mention your name to anyone. But you know what they say. Where there's smoke ..."

That sounds very immature now, I suppose, but I enjoyed seeing her discomfort. They sure weren't considering my comfort when they moved into my neighborhood.

The weather began to clear on Wednesday and my spirits lifted with the clouds. For his part, Curtis was becoming more and more comfortable every day, just as I was more and more accepting of his presence. He was content most of the time lounging on various pieces of furniture and even sought me out occasionally when he was in the mood for some affection.

The next to last day of November was bright and sunny and almost warm. Annette was at my house at 7:30 Thursday morning. She'd brought croissants that we devoured over coffee and strategy. By quarter to nine, we seemed to have every plan in place and every possibility covered. At least, we thought we did.

I turned off the coffee pot and set the thermostat at 65. Linda had agreed to check on the cat once a day. It was time to go.

We were taking two cars—my new Honda and Annette's flashy royal blue BMW convertible.

"I'll check into the motel at the expressway exit," I told her as we stood in the driveway, "and call you with the room number as soon as I have it. Then I guess I'll hang around there. I don't want to risk going back into town and being recognized by Lazenby or one of his people." That he had people wasn't in doubt. After all, he'd had one of them run me off the road.

She gave a quick nod. "I'll get settled in downtown, visit Robin's shop and then we can meet in your room late this afternoon."

Minutes later, we were southbound on Interstate 75. For a little while, we rode in tandem, but then Annette's nature asserted itself. She picked up speed and was soon out of sight.

I amused myself singing along with an Emmylou Harris CD. I sang loud, with great enthusiasm, and thought my harmonies were right on target. My daughter would have been appalled and, somehow, that thought made me smile.

TWENTY-THREE

WITH NORAH JONES PROVIDING THE BACKGROUND MUSIC, AN-
nette steered the peppy little car along the highway, smoothly negoti-
ating the always heavy traffic. No one enjoyed traveling this crowded
interstate, but jammed as it was with trucks and Florida-bound snow-
birds, it was still the quickest and most direct route south from Macon.

Nearly bare trees and brown fields were all there was to be seen
on the sides of the road. She hummed along for a bit with Norah
until her thoughts got the better of her. What was she going to do
about Scott? *She* wasn't unhappy with the situation. In fact, it suited her well. She liked her life compartmentalized and Scott nicely
filled the space she had allotted for affection and distraction.

But he wasn't happy with the way things were. He was ready to
settle down, have kids, and all that went with that picture. And he
couldn't—or wouldn't—understand her fear of how that might
work in black and white Georgia. But she didn't want to contem-
plate her life without him.

She reached Fitzgerald just before one. The downtown streets
were busy with lunchtime business. She registered the fact that it
was an attractive place and, following Emily's directions, she located
the Berry Patch Motel, parked outside the office and went in.

148

"Afternoon." The gray-haired man behind the counter smiled a welcome. "Can I help you?" He didn't sound like a native. His voice was accented by the flat vowels of the Midwest. Maybe a retiree who'd moved south and bought a little business.

"I'd like a room—just for a couple of nights."

She registered as Ramla St. John— she thought that had about the right theatrical tone for the business at hand—and he got busy typing things into a computer, handed her a paper to sign, and asked for a credit card.

"Oh, I'll be paying in cash."

He smiled, but insisted. "I'll still need a credit card to guarantee it until you check out."

Annette smiled the smile that had won over thousands of witnesses and suspects over the past years. "Why don't I just pay for the room in advance now." She pushed nine twenties across the counter. "And I'll pick up anything that's left from that when I check out."

He couldn't have been more cooperative after that, offering her choice of poolside, and first or second floor. She chose a ground level room at the back, overlooking the parking lot and the rear of a Denny's restaurant.

"Just put your tag number there and you're done."

She made up a number and scrawled it on the registration form. She was pretty sure he wouldn't check. He gave her two card keys.

"That's number 118, but you're a little bit early. Not sure if housekeeping has finished your room yet."

"No problem. I'll go out and get some lunch and have a look around town before going to the room."

Annette had lied. She wasn't interested in food right then. Time was short. However, she did stop at a fast food place. In the restroom, she changed from jeans and a sweater into an African-patterned skirt and long-sleeved black jersey top. She bought a cold drink at the counter on her way out.

Robin Lazenby's shop was tucked into the corner of a strip shopping center on the south side of town. A sign over the door read Chakra—A Mystical Shoppe. Annette suppressed a scowl—she had a serious prejudice against people who thought adding a couple of extra letters to a word somehow made it more picturesque.

The interior of the shop (without the extra p and e) was dim and heavily scented with incense or potpourri or some other concoction. Annette wandered around like a curious customer for a few minutes. The sheer amount of inventory was overwhelming. Dresses, capes, blouses, and skirts were jammed onto racks in the back. One wall was devoted to books about witchcraft, tarot cards, feng shui, and other things Annette had never heard of. Magic was frequently used in the names of the products, often spelled with a k. Why couldn't people just operate within the normal range of the language?

There were crystals, candles, jewelry, and polished stones. Many things were labeled with the words Goddess, Celtic, Druid, or Wiccan. The only other customers in the store were two teenaged girls giggling and whispering over a book on witchcraft for teens.

As she was examining a crystal ball on a bronze stand, Annette noticed a woman, presumably the proprietor, emerge from a back room. She was strikingly pretty although her long blonde hair might have better suited a woman a decade or two younger. Her multi-colored silk dress with flowing sleeves and flouncy skirt seemed appropriate for her location. In fact, Annette couldn't imagine anyone wearing such a creation anywhere but a shop such as this or, maybe, as an actor in a Renaissance festival.

"Hi. Welcome to Chakra," she said in a breathy, little girl voice. "I'm Robyn."

"Hello," Annette said, deliberately pitching her voice lower. "You have a very nice place." She kept her eyes on the other woman's and tried to inject a hint of the Caribbean in her voice. It just seemed appropriate. "My name is Ramla St. John." She'd found the first name the night before on a website of African names. It meant prophetess, which seemed appropriate.

"Let me know if I can help you find anything."

Annette just nodded and resumed wandering around the shop, pausing frequently to give Robyn Lazenby long looks.

Robyn noticed, just as she was supposed to. "Is everything okay? You keep looking at me."

Annette nodded. "Yes, yes. It's just that you look familiar to me, but I know we haven't met."

"No," Robyn said. "I'd certainly remember meeting you."

Annette shrugged her shoulders. The two teenagers left without buying anything. She turned her attention to a display of crystals and spent a good ten minutes examining them. While she didn't see much difference among them, she wanted to give the appearance of making a studied choice. Finally, she picked up a pretty polished lavender one, labeled Amethyst Crystal Tower and took it to the cash register.

Robyn smiled her approval. "Oh, yes, the amethyst. Wonderful for repelling negative energy, isn't it?"

"Yes, it is," Annette agreed, having no idea what Robyn was talking about.

The other woman pulled a sheet of tissue paper from beneath the counter and began reverently wrapping the crystal in it, then placed it in a small white paper bag. She punched a few numbers into a calculator. "That'll be $67.25."

Annette almost choked. $67.25 for a *rock*? But she managed to keep her face expressionless. She pulled three twenties and a ten from her bag and handed them over.

Robyn made change, holding out the bills and coins in Annette's direction.

Annette gasped and took a step back. "No, no. I don't want that. You keep it." She did her best to sound as if the money disgusted her. She grabbed the little bag holding the crystal. "I have to go now."

"But what..."

Annette hurried to the door like the hounds of hell were after her.

"Wait! What's the matter?"

Annette turned reluctantly around. "I'm sorry. It's that I just remembered where I saw you. A dream. I dreamed about you. And I... I don't really think I should ... ummm ... be with you. I mean ..."

Robyn rushed toward Annette, her face a mask of alarm. "What do you mean? What did you dream?"

Annette sighed. "It's not you, exactly. But there's a problem with someone close to you. I saw a tall man in my dream—a big, smiling man. But his aura." She shuddered dramatically. "His aura was dark and ... well ... I have to say bloody. He's carrying darkness with him everywhere he goes. And it... it leaches onto those closest to him. You and ... Are there children? Two?"

Robyn was nodding vigorously. "Yes, yes."

"There were two others, weren't there? Taken before they ever drew breath? They, too, were touched by the evil."

Robyn gasped. "How did you know?"

"I don't know. I never know where the knowledge comes from." Annette reached for the door and pushed it open. "Well, I'm sorry for your troubles. But I must leave. Now."

She stepped forward, but was stopped by Robyn's hand on her arm.

"Wait. You can't tell me that and just leave. You have to help me."

Annette gently removed her arm from Robyn's hand. "I don't know that I can," she said sadly. "It may already be too late."

"Couldn't you try?"

She touched her lips with the fingertips of one hand. "I would have to do a reading." She shook her head reluctantly. "It would take so much energy. And there are no guarantees."

"Then do a reading. We could do it right now. I'll close the shop."

"No, no. I'd have to prepare for such a reading; purify myself." She gave Robyn a small, tired smile. "I will try. Perhaps I can help."

"Oh, thank you. When? When can you do the reading?"

"Tomorrow afternoon. I must prepare. As do you. Tomorrow when you rise, take only water and juice. No solid food. Bathe carefully and dress only in natural fibers—nothing synthetic. That's very important now. And pray—pray for God's help."

"I can do that."

"Very well. I will see you here at two tomorrow afternoon."

A second later she was back out in the parking lot. She walked quickly to her car and got in. She took a few shaky breaths. Her heart was pounding. She didn't enjoy undercover work—never had. During the five years she'd worked as a police officer before transferring to the DA's office, she'd had only three undercover assignments. And she'd hated every one. She was much happier when the bad guys knew who she was and she knew who they were.

A glance in her rearview mirror showed Robyn Lazenby standing in the doorway of her shop, fear still showing on her pretty face. Annette reached into her purse for a small pill box. She shook one tiny white tablet out and popped it into her mouth, swallowing without water.

As her heart rate began to slow, she started the car. The first part was over.

TWENTY-FOUR

ANNETTE HAD THE STARRING ROLE IN OUR PRODUCTION, SO I had little to do that afternoon except hang out in the background in case she needed me. Even in a new car, I didn't want to drive into town where I might be recognized. But there was one place I knew I'd be safe—and welcome.

Miss Gene greeted me with a big smile, asked about my knee, and seated me at the kitchen table. She'd just taken two pumpkin pies out of the oven and I was happy to sample one.

"There now," she said, setting a nice big wedge before me, "how about a little whipped cream on top of that?"

I couldn't think of any reason to turn that down, or the coffee she offered to go with it.

"Well, you sure caused a firestorm last time you were here, honey." She plopped whipped cream on my pie and put an equally generous helping on her own. "Jim Lazenby threw a tantrum when he heard you'd practically accused him of trying to kill you! Cheryl Pressley was right there in the office when the police came to talk to him. She told everyone she knew, I guess, 'cause I've heard it from several different folks. And, of course, she told me herself. She comes here pretty regular."

"I didn't think anything would come of making that report."

"Well, nothing did, not really. They put out a description of the man in the pickup that ran you off the road, but without any more information than they had, they didn't find him. And as for Lazenby, the police didn't have any proof he was behind it, but they had to go ask him about it after you told them what you did. And he pitched a fit! Folks heard him yelling clear out on the street. For a while there he was demanding that they arrest you for making a false report."

She poured us both coffee and set cream and sugar on the table.

"Really?" Stranger things had happened in small towns, I knew. I hoped there wasn't an outstanding warrant with my name on it.

"Well, of course they wouldn't do that. Then he demanded to see their reports, especially wanted your name and address. But they wouldn't give him that information either. I mean, they let him see the reports, but they wouldn't give him your address. Told him it was an ongoing investigation. Of course, they didn't arrest him or anything."

I was surprised that a small-town police department would stand up like that to one of their most influencial citizens. Guess it just goes to show you not to make assumptions. It sounded like the officers did everything right. It wasn't surprising that there'd been no arrest. I sure hadn't been able to give them anything to go on.

"After the police left the office, he lit into Cheryl real bad, screaming and calling her names, telling her she had no right to give out any personal information about him. The poor girl tried to tell him she hadn't, but he wouldn't listen. Fired her right there on the spot. I heard she cleared all her things out of her apartment last weekend."

"Wow, no job and no place to live. I'm sorry if I caused that."

"You didn't cause anything, honey. Jim Lazenby is who caused it. And it's not such a bad thing that Cheryl's away from that scoundrel. I expect he'll be looking for a replacement right quick. He does like women."

She sipped her coffee. "Now Cheryl has moved back in with her mama. She's better off there, although I expect she'll have it kind of rough for a while, being pregnant and all." Miss Gene shook her head. "I'm sorry for her troubles. I've always thought she was such a nice girl. So sweet and polite."

She smiled sadly. "After the blow-up, she came out here for something to calm her down. I wasn't about to give her any potion because of the baby, but I gave her a little bag of herbs, mostly lavender, told her to sleep with it under her pillow. And I gave her some advice, too. Told her to think about leaving Fitzgerald for a while—just 'til everything settles down again. There's a lot of talk right now that she shouldn't have to hear. Besides, Jim Lazenby carries grudges. He'll make it as hard as he can for her."

"Is she going to leave?"

"I don't know. She said she wouldn't leave town for anyone, that she wasn't going to run away. But she came by yesterday and got a good luck bag—some herbs and a pretty rock or two." She smiled. "She even brought me a little present." She nodded toward the shelves and smiled. "That purple ceramic frog on the end. I'm pretty sure Cheryl painted it herself. It doesn't look exactly professional and purple's her favorite color."

I wasn't sure, but there might have been a sheen of tears in her eyes. "Cheryl said she wanted to thank me for everything I'd done for her and her mama."

"Maybe she is planning to go away."

"Maybe, but she was still saying no one was going to run her away from her home. Said she had plenty of ammunition herself if Lazenby started anything. She's told me a bunch of times that Lazenby is going to have to take care of her and the baby 'cause she's got something to make him.

"Of course, I don't know what she meant by that. Sure, she could tell people he'd had an affair with her and about the baby and all that, but I don't see what good it would do. I mean, the whole town already knows it."

I had another bite of pie. "Did they ever find the pickup that ran me off the road?"

She shook her head. "Not that I've heard. Had to guess, I'd say that truck is several counties away, being repaired. There's lots of shade tree mechanics around. When it's back here, it'll look good as new and probably be a different color."

Miss Gene had been busy preparing for the coming winter. "We had a good harvest this year. I've put up fifty pints of peas and another forty-five pints of corn. That, with the tomatoes and peaches I canned, ought to see me through to spring."

She showed me the big, neat woodpile in the back yard. "Had a couple of trees fall this summer and one of the Johnson boys came over and chopped 'em up real nice for me." She grinned. "Their mama's looking for a new husband and I gave her some charms and advice in return. I wouldn't be surprised if old Cliff Akins from over in Irwinville didn't come around to see her pretty soon."

I had no doubt that Cliff was destined for matrimony and wondered how Miss Gene had managed that.

Before I left, I asked if she thought Cheryl Pressley might talk to me.

"Oh, I think so. She's already talked to everyone who'll listen. She's mad as all get out right now."

She gave me Cheryl's phone number and directions to the duplex where she lived with her mother.

TWENTY-FIVE

NOW THAT THE TIME HAD CHANGED BACK, THE SUN SET around 5:30. So it was already twilight when I pulled alongside the curb at Vista Gardens, the duplex community outside of town where Cheryl lived with her mother. The complex hadn't been there long, the landscaping still in its beginning stages. The individual single-story units were painted different neutral colors, but splashes of seasonal color broke up the sea of beige, gray, and brown. Almost every yard had beds of pansies or containers of orange and yellow chrysanthemums. The Pressleys lived at 1602. A green Ford Focus was parked in the drive.

Cheryl answered the door herself. She was dressed in jeans and a long-sleeve jersey that was tight enough to show off the beginnings of a tummy.

"Hi, I don't know if you remember me ..."

"I sure do." She didn't seem pleased to see me. "You're the one who caused so much upset around here a few weeks ago. I wouldn't be forgetting *you*."

Nice to be remembered, I guessed. "Uh, could I come in and talk to you?"

She hesitated for a moment, then shrugged. "Sure, why not?"

She stepped back and I entered the small living room. A sofa and chair, covered in a bright floral print, invited visitors to get comfortable and a flat-screen TV dominated one end of the room. The volume was turned down, but animated players on a game show were jumping around in excitement.

"Sit down. You want a diet Coke?"

"No, thanks." I sat on the sofa. "Is your mother here?"

She shook her head. "Up in Atlanta. My aunt's having surgery in the morning."

I jumped right in. "Cheryl, I'm interested in Jim Lazenby."

"He's a snake. Not much else to know except I was a damned fool for listening to his sweet stories."

I decided there was nothing to be gained by being subtle. "He cheated some friends of mine out of a lot of money. I'm trying to get it back."

"He's cheated lots of people. Nobody ever gets nothing back from Jim." She gave me a smile that was part cunning and part excitement. "Until now. I'm going to get my own back."

I guess I glanced sympathetically at her slightly rounded stomach and she caught me.

"You know about the baby, huh?"

"Well, I heard..."

"Yeah, I guess everybody knows. But that ain't what I'm talking about. Think I'd want him havin' anything to do with *my* child? Hell, no. He needs to stay far away from this baby. But I'm still going to make him pay—and pay big."

"I don't understand."

"You don't gotta understand. But he will. He'll understand plenty once I play that recording for him. Ol' Jimmy likes to talk sometimes, likes to show us little girls what a big, tough man he is, especially after he's had a few drinks and a lot of loving. He just didn't expect me to be smart enough to do anything about it."

I didn't like the sound of that. "Listen, he's a dangerous man, Cheryl. You must know that."

She sniffed. She couldn't have been more than 25 and had the conviction that she was bullet-proof that goes along with that age. "What's he gonna do? Can't do nothin' to me long as I got the recording."

"What recording are you talking about?"

Her hand caressed the end table beside her and her eyes got a faraway look. "He's the only one who has to know that. But as long as I got it and he doesn't, I'll be calling the shots. My baby's going to have everything he needs or wants. Mr. Jim Lazenby will see to that."

She picked up a soft drink can from the table and drank from it. Then she smiled. "Yeah, unless he wants to go to jail for a long time, he'll give me what I want. *Then* I'll leave this place, go to Atlanta or New Orleans or somewhere. Might go back to LA. I've got friends there. I'm a singer, you know? A real good one. All I need is to be somewhere I can get a break."

"What about the baby? It'll be hard starting in a new place with a little one."

She thought for a minute. "Maybe so. Or maybe I'll let my mama keep it for a while, 'til I get settled and everything."

I tried again to get her to tell me what was on the tape, but she wouldn't, any more than she'd reconsider trying to get money from Lazenby.

"He *deserves* to pay for how he treated me. And he's going to."

I stayed a few more minutes, doing what I could to discourage her, but finally gave it up.

By 6:30, I was back at the motel. I was considering dinner choices when my cell phone rang.

"How's it going?" Annette asked when I answered.

"Okay. I did a little more snooping, but didn't find out anything that will help us. How about you?"

"Oh, I'm going about, reading minds, putting curses on people—you know, the usual for us psychics."

"Want to come out here and have something to eat? There's a steakhouse down the street that might be good."

"No, we don't want to take a chance on people seeing us together. I think I'm going to have dinner at Carlo's. I want to see this Lazenby guy in the flesh. Isn't that the place your witch said he goes every night?"

"Well, most every night, I think. But how will you recognize him?"

There was a long silent moment until I realized that I'd asked a stupid question. "Oh, yeah, the computer research."

"Yep, there were a lot of pictures of Jimmy-boy online. He does seem to love the cameras. I don't think he'll be too hard to spot."

I tried the steakhouse myself. The meal was good, but I was restless. I wished I were with Annette checking out Lazenby, and I was really worried about Cheryl Pressley. She was so young and really believed that things were going to work out just like she planned. I knew from long experience that rarely happened.

I wanted to be doing something, anything, to help the plan along. Instead, here I was eating prime rib and reading a newspaper.

Back at the motel, the hours stretched out before me. I tried reading, but couldn't get interested in the book I'd brought. I finally turned off the lights early—10:15—but it was a couple of hours before I slept. Just before dropping off, I decided I'd call Cheryl in the morning and try, one more time, to talk some sense into her. I'd even threaten her with the police if I had to.

TWENTY-SIX

ANNETTE TOOK SPECIAL PAINS WITH HER APPEARANCE THAT evening. She chose a long, silky sari of orange and yellow silk shot through with metallic threads. Her long braids were swept up and back and caught in a mahogany clip. She took longer than usual applying her makeup and finished with a bronze lip gloss.

She thought the encounter with Robyn Lazenby had gone reasonably well. Had she been convincing in her show of fear when the other woman offered her change? She hoped so.

One last glance in the mirror gave her a little boost of confidence. She looked good, she knew—exotic and somewhat mysterious. If Robyn accompanied her husband to Carlo's tonight, Annette wanted to look the part she'd already started playing.

It was a 10-minute drive to the restaurant. Annette figured it was probably a 10-minute drive to most anywhere in Fitzgerald. Carlo's was on one of the highways just outside town. Set off by itself, it looked new and sleek with a steeply pitched roof and big carved wood doors at the front.

Annette drew curious stares the moment she walked in the place.

"Just one?" The hostess was a pert little girl, probably still in her teens.

"Yes, just one."

The girl consulted a plastic-covered chart on her table. "Well...we're kind of crowded tonight. Would the bar be okay? You can order dinner there, too."

"The bar would be lovely."

Annette followed her to a small table in the corner of the bar area, turning heads as she passed.

"Is this okay?"

"Fine."

Five minutes later, she was sipping a martini and examining the menu, seemingly unaware of the interest she was causing in the room. The attention she was attracting ranged from curious to admiring and was just what she'd planned. If you're going to be an exotic fortune teller, she reasoned, you ought to look the part.

She gave her order to a nice young man, then sat back and surveyed the room around her. Most of the people there were couples, apparently waiting for tables in the main dining room. However, at one end of the big wooden bar three businessmen in suits, ties loosened, were talking and drinking with no sign of dinner plans. One of them was Jim Lazenby.

His face was flushed and his laugh and voice were louder than the others. While she watched, he looked away from his companions and across the room. When his gaze fell on Annette, his eyes widened with interest. She met his look and held it for a moment—not long enough to be confrontational, but not short enough to indicate fear. There was nothing in his glance that made her think Robyn had told him about her. He seemed intrigued, not antagonistic.

During the meal, which she enjoyed, she was aware of his eyes on her several times, but she never looked back at him. Evidently

Robyn wasn't with him, so her efforts at looking like a gypsy or something were for nothing, but she had gotten a look at the guy.

Dinner over, she was in the lobby, making her way to the door, when Lazenby was suddenly at her side.

He gave her his most disarming smile. "Well, hello, there. Haven't seen you in town before."

She smiled. "Just got here."

"Business or pleasure? We've got some really interesting historical sites here."

"Wish I had time to look around. I'm just here for a few days on business."

Annette edged toward the door. He stuck right with her.

"What kind of business are you in, Miss …?"

"St. John. Ramla St. John."

"Jim Lazenby."

He held out his hand and Annette had no choice but to take it. His grasp was warm, not too hard and lasted about five seconds longer than it should have.

"So, what business did you say you were in?"

"Consulting. I'm thinking of opening an office here."

"Wonderful. We always welcome new business. Where are you staying? Do you have friends or family here?" He held the door open for her and they walked outside.

"No. I'm at the Berry Patch."

"Nice little place. Look, my business is real estate. I'd like to show you around town when you're ready to look for a place to set up shop. I promise I'll get you the best deal in town."

They'd reached her car and Annette clicked the lock open. "That would be very nice, but I haven't really made up my mind."

She opened the door, but Lazenby moved closer, preventing her from getting in. "You know, I'd still like to show you around. Any time you want."

He was close enough that she could smell the bourbon on his breath. He touched her cheek with one finger, rubbing it up and down. It was all she could do not to jerk back in disgust. "I could show you a fine time, Ramla. One you'd never forget."

Forcing a smile, Annette twisted around and dropped into the driver's seat. She looked up at him. "I bet you could, Jim. But really, I'm only here for a short time. Perhaps on my next trip."

He stepped back and allowed her to close the door. She started the engine, then lowered the window and looked up at him. "See you soon."

It wasn't until she was a block away from Carlo's that Annette completely relaxed. The encounter with Lazenby had been entirely too close for her comfort.

Back at her motel, Annette called Scott. She didn't tell him much about what she'd been doing. It was enough to hear his voice, his wonderful normal voice, on a day that had been anything but normal.

TWENTY-SEVEN

ANNETTE AND I MET AT A WAFFLE HOUSE AT AN EXPRESSWAY exit about 20 miles north of my motel just after 8:00.

"I'm starved," she said. "I've been up for hours. Did you know there are chickens wandering all over Fitzgerald? A rooster hasn't woken me up since I was a little girl."

I told her about the chickens while we worked our way through omelets, waffles, and several cups of coffee, and she told me about her encounter with Lazenby.

"Uggh," I said. "He touched you?"

"Yeah, it was kind of like having a lizard lick my cheek."

"Listen, Annette. He's dangerous. I know he is. Be careful around him."

She smiled. "Oh, I think I can handle him. He's no different than a lot of guys we've locked up in the past. So full of himself that he doesn't notice what's going on around him. He's sure he's smarter than anyone else."

"Well, be careful anyway." The waitress poured more coffee into my cup. "So, are you ready to tackle Robyn again?"

"Yeah. I think so. I've practiced that move with the cards so many times I've started dreaming about it. I'm as ready as I'm going to be."

She looked up from her plate and I noticed a bright spot of blood at the bottom of her left nostril.

"What is it, Emily?"

I gestured to my own nose, then pointed to the red trickle. "You're bleeding."

She put a napkin up to her nose, then looked at the blot of blood on it. "Oh, yeah. That's been happening some lately."

"Are you okay?"

She held the napkin to her nose as she spoke. "Yeah, it's nothing. It'll stop soon."

"If you say so," I said uncertainly.

Annette opened a tiny box, shook a white pill into her hand and downed it with a sip of water.

After breakfast, Annette headed back into town. I thought I'd try one more time to discourage Cheryl from what she had planned. I called her number, but got no answer. Maybe I'd be able to talk to her later.

TWENTY-EIGHT

CHAKRA WAS EMPTY OF CUSTOMERS. AS SOON AS ANNETTE entered the shop, Robyn locked the door and turned the little cardboard sign on it to Closed. She'd set up a small table near the back of the store and covered it with a deep blue silk cloth.

"I . . . I hope this is okay. Silk's a natural fiber, isn't it?" Robyn was dressed in dark cotton slacks and a plain white shirt. She was jittery, her hands in constant movement.

"This is satisfactory, but we need four candles."

Robyn hurried to one side of the shop and returned with four small white candles. After Annette placed one on each corner "for the four points of the compass", she had Robyn light them. In moments, the scent of jasmine filled the air.

Annette took a chair on one side of the table, nodded for Robyn to sit opposite her and reached into the cloth tote she carried for the tarot cards she'd borrowed from Linda.

Before beginning, she reached across the table and took Robyn's hands in her own.

"First we pray for protection."

She bowed her head in silence for over a minute, then released Robyn's hands.

"We will begin."

She unwrapped the cards from the silk scarf. She held the deck in her left hand.

"Is that a customer?" she asked, nodding her head toward the front door where a woman walked past.

When Robyn turned to look, Annette removed the bottom cards from the deck, those she'd already arranged. As she'd practiced so many times, Annette set the selected cards, covered with the crumpled scarf, in her lap.

"You must concentrate on the problem at hand," she told Robyn. "The cards will tell us how to combat the evil that has entered your life." As she spoke, Annette shuffled the cards several times.

"Now, Robyn, close your eyes and picture your life." She put the deck on the table before her, then carefully picked up the scarf. "Picture the people in your life and let yourself realize how they affect you. Do they love you?" She placed the scarf on top of the deck, dropping the hidden cards into place. "Do they support you or do they hinder your growth, your freedom? Now open your eyes."

Robyn did so and Annette placed her hands over the scarf and closed her own eyes. "We must pray once more that the energy in these cards will work for you. That your sincerity and true heart will be felt."

Annette bowed her head, wondering how in the world she could speak such gibberish with a straight face. She raised her head, removed the scarf, picked up the deck and dealt the first card. It was a lion with the word Strength written across the top, but it was upside down.

"This covers you. This tells me you are feeling weak and vulnerable." She glanced at the other woman. "Is there perhaps a problem with alcohol or drugs?"

Robyn didn't respond, but her fingertips fluttered along the table top.

Annette placed a second card horizontally across the first. "Ah, the Devil. This crosses you for good or bad. You may be trapped in an oppressive situation, caught in a terrible web of self-imposed bondage. I believe you are in a relationship that is harmful to you and possibly others. Perhaps those others in danger are your two children."

"Yes," Robyn said in a voice barely above a whisper. "My children."

"Ummmhmmm." Annette placed a card below the others. "This, the King of Swords, reversed, is beneath you, your past influences. You have been deceived and exploited by a strong man. He is cruel and cold-hearted and you have been under his influence for a long time."

Robyn nodded.

Annette placed a card to the left of the first ones. She sighed. "Another card in reversal. The Five of Swords. This is behind you. The recent past. There is nothing good here either. Loss, humiliation, intimidation, malicious gossip, suspicion." Annette gave Robyn a pitying look. "You've had a bad time, haven't you?"

Robyn's eyes shone with tears, but she just nodded.

Annette dealt a fifth card and placed it above the others. The appearance of the Death card caused Robyn to draw in a sharp breath.

"This crowns you." Annette concentrated on the script and on keeping that touch of the Caribbean in her voice. "It shows the potential of the situation. Future results. Major change is coming.

In this spread, it's not a positive card and it actually may well mean death — your own or that of someone you know."

Robyn's face had lost its color. She wasn't looking good and Annette had a moment of guilt for causing this woman grief. But she told herself it was for a good cause and went on. The next card, which she placed to the right of the others, was the High Priestess.

"This is before you — circumstances and influences in the near future. And it is a hopeful sign. The Priestess tells us that something positive is going on beneath the surface. There will be spiritual enlightenment."

Linda had told her that the High Priestess also meant that an intuitive woman would come to your aid, but Annette didn't say that. She figured Robyn knew the cards' meanings better than she did.

Annette now started a vertical line of cards to the right of the others she'd laid down. The first card was the Moon.

"This is your self," she said as she put it in place. "This is how you see yourself and your situation. It shows confusion and self-deception. Robyn, you must listen to your intuition. Tap into your psychic awareness and accept the truths you find there. Bring the secrets out into the light."

She laid another above the Moon. "Ummmmmm. The Page of Cups reversed. This is your environment and the people around you. You are living in a fantasy world where you think things are going to get better. You've allowed others to control you. Your laziness and lack of discipline has not only hurt you, but it may be hurting your children. And once again, I see alcohol or drug abuse."

Robyn wouldn't meet her eyes, so Annette went on, "If you are having these problems, you must get help. Otherwise, the death we've seen here may be yours."

"I ... I might need to," Robyn said, "but it's so hard."

"If you try, the strength will be yours and you will succeed."

Annette returned her attention to the cards and placed a third in the vertical line. "This represents your hopes and fears." It showed a big red heart with blood dripping from it where three swords had pierced it. "The heartbreak card, the Three of Swords. You are afraid that sorrow and hurt are coming. And they may. This card can indicate loss, funerals, death, and grieving. And I think your fear is well founded.

"It all depends on the outcome card." She laid down the last card in the spread and Robyn gave a little cry when she saw it. It was the Tower of Destruction, showing a medieval-looking tower, struck by lightning, with people falling from it. "This is what is to come. It's the most likely result of your situation. And the Tower, of course, means violent destruction of your old way of life. The deeper your self-deception, the deeper the change will be. And, like several of the other cards, the Tower can also mean death."

Robyn buried her face in her hands for a moment. When she raised her head, her eyes, wet with tears, darted from card to card in the spread before her.

"It's ... I've never seen such a negative spread." She sounded close to panic.

"It is bad, but we must consider what your options and alternatives are. The cards are never set in stone. You *can* change the outcome if you're willing to do what is necessary."

"I am!"

Annette nodded in what she hoped was a wise way. "Then there is hope. Let us look at the cards as a whole. What do you see?"

"Everything bad! Death and destruction and bad luck!"

"Yes, but we must try and determine where the cause of all this lies. There are, of course, four suits in the tarot deck."

Robyn nodded. "That's right. Cups, swords, wands, and pentacles."

"Yes. Now consider this spread. What suits do you see?"

Robyn stared at the cards. "Ummmm... the three swords and one cups."

"That's right. Swords typically represents people who are aggressive, insensitive, and calculating. And astrologically, the Swords suit is related to Gemini, Libra, and Aquarius. When were you born, Robyn?"

"April 20."

"So, the swords cards don't represent you. When was your husband born?"

"October 2." She swallowed hard. "He's a Libra."

"I feel that the dire outcomes in the spread are due to your husband. I sense that he's a controlling, cruel man whose deceptive dealings have brought suffering to many. His actions will bring calamity to him and his family. You will all suffer."

"I knew it," Robyn said miserably, her face twisted with fear. "I knew there was a curse. What can we do?"

"Nothing will save your husband. His doom is certain. But there's a chance you and your children will survive and might even prosper.But there must be an offering. A sacrifice. What numbers do you see on the swords cards in the spread?"

"There aren't many. There's a three and over here is a five."

"Yes, a three and a five. The total is eight and must be the sacrifice. Eight thousand dollars."

"You mean give it to *you?*" Robyn asked, suspicion creeping into her voice.

"No, no." Annette did her best to sound horrified. "I won't even touch it. We will destroy it together. We'll burn it."

Annette hoped she'd be able to pull off the sleight of hand trick it would take to accomplish that little task. She'd been practicing that for days, too.

"*Burn it?*"

"Yes, it must be completely destroyed. It is a symbolic sacrifice, of course, because your husband must have been acquiring his tainted wealth for many years. But it isn't necessary to destroy it all.

"But we must be quick. I just hope it's not too late. Can you get the money today?"

Robyn looked uneasy. "Yes, I *guess* I can get it."

"Then here is what you must do. After I leave, go to your bank and withdraw the money." She reached into the tote and brought out an oversized pale blue envelope. She had its twin back at her hotel room, already stuffed with paper cut to the size of hundred-dollar bills. "Touch it as little as possible. Put it into this envelope and seal it immediately. Tell no one about this.

"At 5:00, bring it to my room — number 118 at the Berry Patch Motel. Do not stop anywhere along the way. I will have purified the room with sage and incense by the time you arrive. Together we will pray and then try to rid your family of this curse."

Robyn still looked terrified, but she nodded. "I'll do it."

Annette took Robyn's hands one last time. "After the curse has been eradicated, you and your children can get on with your lives, but you have a much better chance of succeeding if you leave your husband."

She placed the cards back in her bag. "Hurry. The waiting evil gains strength with every moment that passes. It must be done as quickly as possible."

"I'll go right now."

TWENTY-NINE

I'D TRIED CALLING CHERYL PRESSLEY SEVERAL TIMES, BUT still hadn't been able to talk to her. Of course, she could have been visiting friends or out shopping, but I was getting more uneasy by the moment. Was this the day she'd chosen to make her move against Lazenby? I hoped not. If I could find her, maybe I could talk the whole plan. Finally, after a late lunch, I climbed into my car and went to find her.

It was a beautiful autumn day, a good ten to fifteen degrees warmer than it would be at home. I let the windows down and enjoyed the fresh air. Vista Gardens was alive with kids that afternoon, fresh from school and full of energy. Their shouts and laughter filled the air. The same green Ford was parked in the Pressleys' driveway. Cheryl must have just gotten home.

I rang the bell, but no one answered. After a minute or two, I rang again and knocked. The blinds were closed, keeping me from seeing into the front room.

I went around the building, thinking I was going to feel pretty foolish if Cheryl was just off with a friend, but I couldn't quiet the uneasiness. There was a small patio attached to the back of the Pressleys' unit, and a sliding glass door. Cupping my hands to cut the glare, I peered into the apartment. I could see the kitchen and, towards the front, a slice of the living room. But it didn't resemble the neat, orderly place I'd visited the day before. There were papers and magazines on the floor and a lamp lay broken beside the sofa.

I tried the door and found it was unlocked. It slid open silently. Before entering, I slipped my gun out of my purse and held it down by my leg. I wasn't going to be caught unarmed a second time.

Cheryl Pressley was sprawled on the floor in front of the television. Two soap opera actresses argued on the screen. Cheryl was completely still. It looked like she'd been stabbed. Blood had flowed from several wounds on her torso and formed a pool around her. The edges of the puddle were beginning to dry. I put the gun away. Whoever did this was long gone.

Knowing it was futile, I still moved behind her head, careful not to step in the blood, and felt for a pulse in her neck. There was nothing, of course. Her skin was cool to the touch. She'd been dead for hours, maybe since the night before.

I got to my feet and surveyed the room as best I could. There was no sign of a weapon. The place had been searched and the little drawer in the end table that she'd glanced at the day before had been pulled out and was laying on the floor. It didn't take any great leap of deduction to know that Jim Lazenby had killed this woman and taken the recording she held over him as blackmail.

The right thing to do was call the police that second, but I didn't. I knew they'd spend time, maybe hours, questioning me. The process could take the rest of the day. I didn't begrudge them doing their jobs, but I had to think first about Annette.

Her meeting with Robyn Lazenby would be over by this time. Everything might go according to plan, but I couldn't just assume that it would, especially now. Lazenby had killed Cheryl and, if his wife had given him any indication that Annette could be a threat, he wouldn't necessarily stop there.

What had I touched? Other than poor, dead Cheryl, I didn't think I'd laid a hand on anything but the back door. I used a dish tower to wipe my prints off the door, then dropped it on the patio. Finally, trying to look as if I belonged there, I walked quickly back to my car, got in, and drove away.

Even though I wasn't going to hang around, Cheryl couldn't lay there waiting to be found by her poor mother. I wasn't sure the Fitzgerald Police 911 system could track a call back to my cell, but it was likely they could. As soon as I was back on the main road, I started looking for a pay phone. Pay phones are pretty much a thing of the past now and I drove by five different convenience stores before I spotted one. It only took a couple of minutes to call the police and suggest they check the Pressleys' place for a body.

Back in the car, I pulled my own phone from my purse and called Annette. There was no answer, just the same empty ringing I'd gotten when I called Cheryl Pressley earlier in the day. It was nearly 5:00. I headed for the Berry Patch Motel with my heart racing, praying I wasn't too late.

THIRTY

ANNETTE TOOK A QUICK SHOWER WHEN SHE GOT BACK TO her room. She felt dirty, like she'd been elbow-deep in some kind of nasty muck. And, she guessed, she had. She didn't enjoy deceiving someone as pathetic as Robyn Lazenby. It was mean, kind of like teasing a child. She tried to convince herself it was for the greater good.

She dried off and pulled on the caftan she'd worn the day before. Then she checked to make sure everything was in place for the final act. She'd dragged one of the bedside tables out into the middle of the room and covered it with a brown-and-gold paisley shawl. A heavy copper bowl and a single fat white candle were the only things on the table top. Two small side chairs completed the arrangement.

She'd already prepared an envelope, identical to the one she'd given Robyn Lazenby, filling it with cut paper which she hoped would feel like cash. Now she slipped it into the voluminous pocket of her caftan. Although she'd practiced and practiced the move, she still wasn't absolutely confident she'd be able to pull it off.

The heavy curtains were closed and one by one Annette switched off the lights and lit the candle. With the flickering flame providing the only light in the darkened room, she thought she just might be able to successfully switch the envelopes without Robyn seeing it.

She strapped on her watch—it was just after 5:00—then checked her phone and saw that Emily had called while she was in the shower. She started to call her back, but stopped when a knock sounded at the door.

Robyn had wasted no time in getting to the bank. Annette took a deep breath, consciously getting back into the Ramla character, then opened the door.

Jim Lazenby had a bottle of Scotch in one hand and a big smile on his face.

"Hello, darlin'." He raised the bottle. "How about a little drink?"

Annette recoiled as if she'd encountered a snake up close. Lazenby's cheeks were flushed and his eyes shiny. She realized he'd already had a fair amount to drink.

"Umm … no, thank you. Not right now. I was just leaving…"

He didn't wait for her to finish, just shouldered his way in and closed the door behind him. Annette stumbled back, thrown slightly off balance by his rough entry.

"What's the hurry? Let's talk for a little while."

"Really, I do need to leave," Annette said, starting to reach around him for the door.

He stepped forward so that his face was only an inch or so from hers. The big smile had disappeared.

"Why would you want to leave? Aren't you waiting for my stupid wife to come and give you a big wad of cash?"

His breath was whiskey sour. She tried to back away, but he grabbed her arm. Her heart was pounding. Her chest was tight and it was hard to take a deep breath. She tried to pull away, but he tightened his grip.

"Whoa. Where do you think you're going?"

"I need one of my pills. They're in my purse."

But he didn't relax his grasp. "I don't think you need anything but a drink, honey. And some straight talk."

He pulled one of the chairs over and shoved her into it, giving the table top with the candle and copper bowl an amused look.

"Is that how you were going to fool the ignorant bitch? Gonna *burn* all that money?" He picked up the bowl and threw it across the room where it bounced off a wall with a metallic clang. "How dumb do you have to be to fall for that shit? That con was old when I was a kid. But Robyn, yeah, Robyn will fall for anything if you pile enough mystical crap on it."

He unscrewed the top of the bottle and took a long swallow. Then he held it out to Annette, but she turned her head away.

"Suit yourself. But you'll probably like what happens next a whole lot more if you're a little loose." He took another swallow. "Where was I? Oh, yeah, my sweet little wife. Goddamn, sometimes I wonder how she manages to feed and dress herself she's so dumb.

"She was actually going to take money out of the bank—out of *my* bank account—and bring it to you to have the curse on our house removed."

"How did you find out?" Annette asked. She was so breathless by now that the question came out in a whisper. She coughed to try and clear her airways, but it didn't help much.

"The teller took the request to the bank vice president. After all, that's a lot of money for anyone to just waltz in and withdraw at the window. He called me, of course."

"But isn't the account in her name as well as yours?"

"Sure, but this is *Robyn* we're talking about here. Hell, I doubt she's ever withdrawn more than $200 at one time in her life. If she needs something, she either pulls out that Visa card or asks me for it. So they called me."

He shook his head at the stupidity. "The bank's right across the street from my office, for God's sake. I was there in two minutes and the fool was still standing at the teller's window waiting for her money. It didn't take long to find out what was going on."

"Is ... is she okay?"

"Who? Robyn? Hell, yes, she's okay. She's home and has probably worked her way through a pitcher of martinis by now." He gave her an ugly grin. "So that just leaves you and me."

He lifted the bottle again, then reached down to jerk Annette to her feet. "I do insist you have a drink with me." He pressed the bottle to her lips and tilted it. The liquor ran down her chin.

"No," she said, trying to pull away. "Just leave. Get out of here. I need to take one of my pills — right now. I'm having trouble breathing." She had another spasm of coughing.

"You look like you're okay to me."

Her cell phone rang, but he didn't release her arm.

She twisted her wrist so she could see her watch. "I need to get that."

"I don't think so. We have to talk about you and your little plan. Did you really think you could take eight thousand dollars from me? I'm sure as hell not about to be taken by some cheap con artist. But I don't mind taking a little something from you. Why don't you get out of that long dress and let's see what we've got here?"

He leaned forward to kiss her. She tried to turn her head, but he grabbed and twisted her long braids, then crushed his mouth against hers, trying to open her lips with his tongue. When he pulled back, he was smiling again.

"I'll give you credit for trying though. It was a good plan, considering how gullible Robyn can be. But it's over. Now let's see how good a loser you are."

He grabbed her arm and began pulling her toward the bed. "You and me are going to have a party, little girl. It can be fun for both of us or… if you don't want play… it can just be fun for me. I figure I deserve some sort of compensation for the trouble you've put me to."

"No! Let me go. If you don't I'll…"

Annette's knees suddenly buckled. She gave a hard, loud gasp and grabbed at her chest. Then crumpled to the floor between the two beds as if her bones had turned to powder.

"What the hell do you think…"

Lazenby leaned forward to look at the woman's still form. She wasn't breathing. He reached down to touch her, but stopped when he heard someone opening the door.

THIRTY-ONE

IT WAS FIVE AFTER FIVE WHEN I PULLED INTO THE BERRY Patch Motel and found a parking place a few doors up from Annette's room. Before I could get out of the car, I saw Jim Lazenby approaching her door. He knocked, Annette opened it and after a moment's conversation, he shouldered his way in and the door closed behind him.

My first impulse was to run to the room, to protect my friend. But I held back. Annette was no helpless little girl. She was a professional who knew how to take care of herself. So I waited.

I scanned the parking lot, but there was no sign of Robyn Lazenby. Was she inside, too? If she showed up now, presumably with the cash Annette had instructed her to bring, I'd have to distract her somehow.

So I waited, glancing at my watch every thirty seconds or so. Finally, I fished the phone out of my bag and punched in Annette's number. After six rings it went to voicemail and I disconnected. I only waited a minute before approaching the room.

I quickly inserted the card key Annette had given me. The little light on the handle flashed green and I opened the door.

It was dark in the room, but a candle provided enough light to see Annette sprawled on the floor beside the bed at Jim Lazenby's feet.

"What did you do to her?" My voice was a controlled scream.

His eyes were wild. "Nothing! I didn't do a damn thing! She just dropped."

I pulled the small revolver out of my pocket and pointed it at him. "Get over there. Over there by the bathroom and don't you move or I'll shoot your ass!"

As he did so, I moved to kneel beside Annette. There was no rise and fall of breathing and she was absolutely still. With my heart pounding in my throat, I reached out and touched the side of her neck with two fingers. It was the second time that day I'd performed the same action.

"She's dead!" I told him. "What did you *do*, you son of a bitch?"

"Nothing! Listen, it's the truth. She just collapsed, like all the air had been let out of her."

"Oh, sure, a healthy young woman just suddenly died and you just happened to be here." I stood up and reached for the phone by the bed. "We'll see if the police believe you because I sure as hell don't."

"Wait." He started toward me, but stopped when I motioned him back with the gun. "I swear that's what happened. She ... yeah, I remember she was complaining that she didn't feel good. She wanted to take a pill or something. So she must have already been sick."

"Then I'm sure that's what their investigation will show. The police will sort it out." I started to punch 911 on the phone.

"Stop! Just don't call. I ... I can't be here." His face was growing redder by the minute and his breath came in quick gasps. "I'm an important man in this town. I can't be found in this room. Listen, I'll just leave and then you can call, okay?"

I looked at him like the slug he was. "You're crazy if you think you're walking out that door, Lazenby. I don't know what you did to her, but you're going to pay for it."

Sudden realization showed in his face. "You're in it with her, aren't you?"

I didn't say anything. Just stood there, holding the phone in one hand and the gun in the other.

"I know you. You're the bitch who was here asking questions about me." A sly look came into his eyes. "You were in this with the fortune teller there."

"You should watch your mouth when someone is pointing a gun at your gut. Some people are sensitive." I gave a humorless laugh. "But yeah, we were working together. Until you killed her."

"I didn't kill her! Look there has to be some way to work this out. Right now neither of us is going to get anything out of this situation. How can we change that?" I watched him deliberately calm himself. The shrewd businessman was coming back to the surface. "How can we work this out?"

I let my gun hand relax a bit and considered what he was saying. "Well, you're right that everybody loses the way things are now." I glanced down at Annette's body. "Maybe she *was* sick. I know she's been popping some kind of pills lately."

"Yeah," he agreed eagerly. "She was coughing bad just before she died."

"I guess you *could* just leave. If you're careful, nobody'd ever know you were even here."

"Oh, I'll be careful all right," he said.

He took two steps toward the door before I stopped him.

"Ummhmm. That would work out just fine for you, but I don't see what it does for me." I gave him a long look. "I came here to make some money, you know."

"It was a stupid plan. I don't know how either of you figured to get away with it. Robyn might be a ditz, but how did you think you'd get around me?"

"Really doesn't matter now, does it? But if I let you walk out of here, I'm left with nothing but a dead body. This whole thing wasn't cheap to set up, you know. It seems like you win and I lose."

A car drove past in the parking lot and Lazenby's eyes cut nervously to the curtained window. "So what do you want to do?" he asked quickly. "Let's get this over with. I want to get out of here."

I took a deep breath. "I can take care of this. The body will disappear and I'll make everything go away for $10,000."

"Are you crazy? Where would I get that kind of money this time of day? The banks are closed." He narrowed his eyes. "'Course I could get it easy first thing in the morning."

"So you think we should just wait here until then?"

"Hell no, I don't. I've got to get out of here. But I could meet you tomorrow, somewhere outside of town. Give it to you then."

I laughed. "Oh, sure. That's going to happen. Once you're out that door, I don't get shit and I know it. No, I want the money right now."

"Again," he said with an exaggerated show of patience, "where do think I could get $10,000 *right now*?"

"Maybe from the trunk of your car?"

His mouth dropped in surprise.

"What's the matter, Jim? Don't you think we did our homework? I probably know more about you than your mama does. And one of the things I know is that you collect your rent money on the first of every month — in cash. And it all goes in that briefcase in the trunk of your car.

"Now this is the first of the month and I know you've been out collecting all day. I'll bet there's at least $10,000 in your trunk."

His shoulders sagged a bit. "Maybe."

"Why don't we go see? But first, step back over there next to the bed." I moved toward the bathroom and gestured with the gun. I eased my cell phone out of my pocket. "Right there in front of my friend."

"What the hell — You're not going to call the police now, are you? Why?"

"Just do what I say."

"Crazy bitch." He moved where I directed, but carefully avoided looking at Annette.

I held up the cell and pressed a button. The room was briefly illuminated by the flash and I checked the screen to make sure Lazenby was recognizable and Annette's body was in the frame.

"Are you out of your fucking mind? What's wrong with you?"

"Just a little insurance. If you've got any thoughts about taking off once we're outside, I'll start screaming bloody murder. You might still drive away, but not before a bunch of people see you. That plus my testimony, the fingerprints you surely left all over this room and the photo ought to be enough to involve you up to your neck. Now let's go get my money."

I picked up a canvas carryall from the dresser, emptied the books it held onto the bed, then opened the door. Lazenby went out.

After I eased the gun back into my pocket, I followed him out to his car. He glanced nervously around, then opened the trunk. The briefcase was there, just as Danny Cooper said it would be.

"What if somebody sees us?"

"The quicker you get me that money, the less chance there is of that."

He opened the case to show piles of cash, neatly stacked inside.

"Count it where I can see it."

He did so, dropping bill after bill into the carryall. It took longer than I'd thought it would, but I stood next to him, watching every move. I didn't like being that close to a murderer, but I wanted to be sure of the amount.

"Satisfied?" he asked when he'd finished.

"Yeah, I'm satisfied."

Once I had the bag in my hand, he slammed the trunk shut. I stepped away from him and put my hand on the gun.

"I don't ever want to see you or hear about this again," he told me. "It would be a real bad mistake for you to ever come back to Fitzgerald."

I believed him. "Don't worry. This is it. You won't hear anything from me again."

"I better not." He opened the driver's door. But before he got in, he asked, "So how are you going to do this? The body, I mean?"

"You don't have to worry. I've got people I can call. Like I told you, the problem will disappear."

He climbed into the car and drove off without ever looking back.

When he was out of sight, I went back into the room, closed the door, and flipped on the light by the door.

"He's gone."

"Thank God," Annette said, sitting up. "I wasn't sure how much longer I could stay there. My right arm is completely numb." She grabbed her purse on the bed, opened it, and pulled out a bright red inhaler. She uncapped it, put one end in her mouth and took two quick puffs from it. She exhaled and smiled. "That's better. Got a little asthmatic there just before I took my fall. But it made the whole thing look more authentic."

THIRTY-TWO

I LOOKED HER UP AND DOWN. "ARE YOU OKAY?"

"Yeah, I'm good now." She twisted her neck in a circular motion. "But I may not be able to move tomorrow. When I dropped the way I did, I ended up in a super uncomfortable position. And I'm so glad you came in when you did. I wasn't sure how much longer I could hold my breath. I was scared to death he was going to touch me." She got to her feet and indulged in a full body stretch.

"I can't believe it worked," I told her, sinking down on the bed. It was the first time I'd relaxed all day. "Just like we planned. I know I was supposed to wait exactly one minute from the time I called your phone, but it was all I could do not to come tearing in here as soon as I saw Lazenby go through the door. I was terrified he'd hurt you!"

She laughed. "Yeah, me, too. And just before I fell, I couldn't remember if I was supposed to time it from the first ring or the last." She shook her head. "Whatever. It's done."

I upended the carryall so that the cash fell out on the bed. "Yeah and we got what we came for. Although it cost a lot more than I thought it would."

"What do you mean?"

But I just shook my head. There'd be time later to tell her about Cheryl. "Let's save the rehash for later. We've still got a lot to do."

"Like what? Let's just go."

"Ummmm. I don't think that's such a good idea. Lazenby is probably feeling safe right about now. He got away from here without being seen — at least as far as he knows. But wouldn't he want to be sure everything was taken care of? I mean, that's what he paid me for. He can't afford to have me walk out and leave your body here, not with his prints all over the room."

She nodded. "Yeah, you're probably right. Wouldn't surprise me if he was parked up the street, just watching to see what happens. So I sure as hell can't walk out of here on my own."

I was already punching a number into my phone. "Then you'll be glad to hear I've planned for that possibility." The phone rang twice before it was answered.

"Danny? It's Emily. We're ready. Room 118."

"On the way."

"Did you remember to cover your license plate?"

"Yes, ma'am. Smeared it real good with mud. And me and Stacy have got hats and big coats to wear. We'll be disguised okay, I think."

They arrived fifteen minutes later and backed the pick-up into a parking space right in front of the room. I let them in the door. They each wore thick coats and sweatpants, and Stacy's long hair was pinned up under a baseball hat. Danny wore some kind of hunting cap. I thought that, at a distance, they probably looked like two big, husky guys.

"It's done," I told them, handing the carryall to Stacy. "There's $9,000 in there for you. We kept $1,000 for expenses."

Tears shone in her eyes. "I don't know how you thought this

up, Miss Emily. And I don't know how we can ever thank you." She smiled at Annette. "Both of you."

"You should be discreet with that money," Annette said. "You don't want to attract any attention and have it get back to Lazenby."

"You don't have to worry about us," Danny said. "We'll be real careful, won't do anything about a new house for a good long while."

"I'm glad we could help," I told them. "But right now we need to finish the job."

Danny had brought a quilt and was spreading it across the bed. He turned his attention to Annette. "Okay, now, if you'll just lay down here, we'll wrap you up and get you into the back of the truck."

Annette grimaced. "I'm not crazy about being wrapped up in a quilt and tossed in a truck."

"It's either that or we have to put you in the trunk of my car," I told her with a grin.

"I guess a quilt doesn't sound so bad."

"It'll be okay, I think," Danny told her. "I made a pallet of blankets back there for you so it'll be nice and soft to lay on."

We rolled Annette up in the quilt and Danny carried her out, settling her gently on the pallet he'd made. I stashed Annette's one bag in my car. Stacy climbed into the truck and Danny got behind the wheel of Annette's BMW. We left the motel and went different directions through town, driving aimlessly around for fifteen minutes or so, making certain we weren't followed.

It was almost eight o'clock when I pulled into the Coopers' driveway. The other three were standing there waiting for me, grins on their faces.

"We did it!" Annette said. She looked gorgeous, as usual. Being wrapped in a quilt and bounced around in a pick-up evidently agreed with her.

We exchanged congratulations, thanks and high fives, all feeling pretty accomplished.

"Y'all want to come in?" Stacy asked. "I can cook us up some supper. I'm starving and you must be, too."

It was tempting. I *was* hungry, but declined. "No, we better get going. The more miles we can put between us and Lazenby the better."

After they both hugged us and thanked us again, Annette and I headed north. On the interstate, she stayed right behind me as the miles rolled past in the darkness. I felt like we might have made it, but I wasn't confident enough to stop until we reached the other side of Macon. Then I called Annette's cell and suggested we find a place to eat.

We ordered hamburgers at the counter of a chain restaurant and took our food to a window booth.

"You sure you're okay?" I asked Annette.

"Yeah, fine." She frowned and brushed her nose with her fingertips then looked at them. "My nose isn't bleeding again, is it?"

"No, it's fine."

She opened her little pill box and popped a white one into her mouth, washing it down with her coffee. "My allergies are about to kill me this year. That's why the asthma is kicking up a little. It was pretty much over at home, but down here the ragweed must still be going strong."

"Is that what's causes the nosebleeds?"

"Not exactly. They're caused by the nose spray I use to treat the allergies. It dries out the inside of my nose." She shook her head, making her braids dance. "If it's not one thing it's another. But it's all good. If allergies are the worst thing I have to endure, I'm really lucky."

We dug into our burgers and fries as if we hadn't eaten for three days.

"Thank the lord for Plan B," Annette said when our pace of eating had slowed.

"Yeah. Plan A was pretty shaky from the start," I agreed.

"Yeah. I mean, how absurd can you get? A curse? Give me a break." She took a bite of fry. "But you know, it almost worked."

"Really?"

"Yeah. Poor Robyn went right to the bank to get the money for me, but somebody called Jim. He was there before she got the cash."

I took a deep breath. "Whatever happened, it worked out okay. Except for Cheryl Pressley."

I told her about the young woman's blackmail plans and murder.

"Is there anything to connect Lazenby to it?"

"Don't think so," I told her. "I'm sure there's going to be plenty of suspicion, but I didn't see anything there that would convict him of the crime. I mean, even if they prove the baby she was carrying was his, that won't really be a big surprise. Everybody in town seems to have known about him and her."

"It's sad," Annette said.

"Yeah, and it probably wouldn't have happened if I hadn't been in Fitzgerald poking around in Lazenby's business. She wouldn't have been fired and she wouldn't have tried to blackmail him."

"You can't know that," she said.

I took in a deep breath and let it out slowly. "Yeah, I can."

When we walked out in the parking lot, I gave Annette $500,

her share of our expense money. She tucked it in her purse, gave me a quick hug and got in her car. Two minutes later we were both driving back on I75. Then she sped up. Her taillights disappeared a couple of minutes later.

During the drive home, I kept replaying the events of the past weeks, imagining how different things might have been if I'd never gone to Fitzgerald. Sure, the Coopers wouldn't have gotten their money back, but Cheryl Pressley might have still been alive. The logical side of my mind insisted that it was only a matter of time before Lazenby discarded Cheryl, just as he had the other women with whom he'd been involved, and that she'd been planning the blackmail long before I arrived on the scene. Making the recording was evidence of that. So maybe her conflict with Lazenby would have happened anyway. That should have made me feel better, but it didn't.

There was also another nagging thought that surfaced from time to time. Would Jim Lazenby be willing to let us get away with it? He knew my name, thanks to the earlier police report. With his contacts, it probably wouldn't be hard for him to get my address.

I didn't see what he'd gain by coming after me, but could his ego stand losing that money? I'd have to be particularly careful for a while.

THIRTY-THREE

ANNETTE PUT THE KEY IN THE LOCK AND TURNED IT. THE dogs were there, prancing around her and turning in excited circles, by the time she got inside. She dropped to one knee and allowed them to greet her properly.

"In a minute," she told them, standing up. "I'll take you out in just a minute."

She deposited her purse on the kitchen counter, but didn't take off her coat. It was so good to be home and safe. She'd never admit it to anyone, but those few minutes in the motel room with Jim Lazenby had been terrifying. Yes, everything went according to plan, but it could just have easily gone horribly wrong.

She shook herself, trying to put it behind her, and turned her attention to the note left by Karen Hoffsteder, the pet sitter who looked after the dogs whenever Annette had to be away from home. There had been no problems and both dogs had been well-behaved, which was exactly what Annette expected.

She retrieved their leashes from a hook on the wall, starting another round of excited prancing. "Karen says you were very good while I was gone, so we'll have an extra long walk tonight." She hooked them up and they nearly dragged her through the door.

The streets were late night quiet as Annette allowed the dogs to lead her along the sidewalk and into the small park across the street. While they tried to sniff every tree and bush in the area, Annette's mind kept running through the events of the day, especially the time with Jim Lazenby. She couldn't remember ever feeling so *alone*.

A gust of wind made her pull her coat tighter. She felt over-dressed with the caftan swishing between her legs. When she took it off tonight, she planned to throw it straight into the trash. She never wanted to wear it again.

"Come on, guys, let's head back."

The dogs were reluctant, but obedient and they started back home. At the instant she stepped into the elevator, dogs pacing around her, Annette had the unpleasant realization that, if Lazen-by had killed her the way he had Cheryl Pressley, there were very few people who'd truly mourn her passing. Sure, her mother would grieve, as would two or three close friends, but that was about it. For everyone else, colleagues and acquaintances, her death would be a sad event, but not something that would have a lasting effect on their lives.

The situation was of her own making, of course. She'd spent most of her adult life concentrating on her career and avoiding getting too involved with other people. You couldn't be hurt if you kept everyone at arm's length. But she realized that she didn't want to settle for that anymore.

When the dogs were let off their leashes, they ran to the kitch-en to see if food might have appeared in their bowls during their absence. Annette slipped off her coat, pulled her phone from her pocket and dialed Scott's number. Her heart began beating hard when he answered.

"I'm back."

"Did you have a good trip?"

She took a deep breath. "It was a tough couple of days. I'll tell you about it when I see you. But... Scott is it too late for you to come over?"

"It *is Friday* night and I don't have to be in the office tomorrow," he said in a voice that sounded as if he could be persuaded.

"Please, could you come?"

"Well, I guess so, but what's so important?"

She smiled. "I just want to be with the man I love."

There was a long moment of silence. Then Scott said, "I'm on my way."

THIRTY-FOUR

I COULDN'T REMEMBER EVER BEING SO HAPPY TO GET HOME.
Curtis greeted me at the door. I fed him and, when I crawled between the covers a little later, he climbed onto the bed with me. I distinctly heard him purring before I fell asleep and realized the time for finding him another home was long gone. He was my cat now and we both seemed content with the state of affairs.

Saturday was filled with the usual weekend chores, like laundry and vacuuming. Now I had a new daily task—scooping out Curtis's litter box. Just past noon I called Linda at her shop to thank her for taking care of the cat.

"Oh, he wasn't a bit of trouble. You know, I think he's warming up to me. He let me scratch his head. Oh, hold on a sec."

As I waited for her deal with a customer, I glanced over at Curtis sprawled on his back in a patch of sunlight. I reflected that his behavior had probably been due more to the fact that he understood Linda was the food dispenser than any warming up on his part, but I didn't voice that suspicion to her.

"Okay, I'm back. So how was Fitzgerald?"

"We got what we went for, but I'm sure glad to be home. Do you want to come over for dinner tonight? It's the least I can do to pay you back for pet sitting."

"Oh, I wish I could, but I've got a class tonight — past life exploration. Hey, why don't you come with me?"

"Ummmm ... I don't think I'm up for that tonight."

"Well, whatever you do, you be careful. There was another robbery in the neighborhood yesterday. Up in the Arbors."

I'd given up trying to teach people the difference between burglary and robbery. "What was taken this time?"

"Not much, I don't think. I heard it was just a jar of change and a bottle or two of wine. But that's not the point, Emily. There are criminals roaming our streets. None of us is safe!"

"I don't think it's that bad," I told her. "I mean it's only been petty thefts, hasn't it? I still think it's probably somebody's grandchildren."

"What about the flasher? Have you forgotten him? I'm not sure I even want to keep living in Marchpoint, what with criminals and sexual predators running loose everywhere. I think I need to go back to the range and practice some more."

We decided to get together for lunch on Sunday. I was hoping to talk her out of keeping that gun. I loved Linda like a sister, but the thought of her with a weapon was truly frightening. Talk about armed and dangerous!

The rest of the day stretched out before me in long, boring hours. Usually I was happy to be by myself, but today I wanted company. Maybe it was the hangover from all the activity of the last two days.

Late that afternoon, I heard Nick Buckley's motorcycle roar into the cul de sac. On an impulse, I phoned him a few minutes later with an invitation to dinner.

"I've checked the fridge and I've got everything we need for a cheese and bacon quiche, unless you're too manly to eat that."

"Hell, no. I love quiche. Soufflés, too." He laughed. "In fact, I'll eat pretty much anything put in front of me. But why don't we go out instead. That way we'll both have plenty of energy for later."

My stomach gave a funny little flip and I could feel heat in my face. "Energy for what?"

He chuckled. "For whatever happens."

We had dinner at the Baconsfield Grill, a nearby casual place frequented by Marchpointers. I started telling him about Fitzgerald over martinis and didn't finish the story until we were halfway through our entrees. Nick had ordered a bottle of wine, a deep red one, and I didn't turn it down.

He'd put down his fork and was staring at me with something that might have been admiration, but was more likely astonishment that a sensible woman would have indulged in such a foolhardy enterprise.

"Damn, Emily Christopher. You pulled it off! You really pulled it off."

"Well, to be fair, *Annette and I* pulled it off."

He shook his head. "It's incredible. I don't even know how you came up with that plan." Then he frowned. "But aren't you concerned that this Lazenby might come after you?"

"No, not really," I said with more conviction than I felt. "He couldn't expect to get the money back, could he? He paid me for a service and got what he wanted. He managed to avoid being mixed up in an ugly mess in the town where he's hoping to run for office. Besides, he knows I have that picture. Why would he come after me?"

"Revenge?" He took a sip of wine.

I shook my head. "I don't think so." I hoped I was right. "I just wish there was some way they could prove that he murdered Cheryl Pressley."

"Would it help if you told them about your conversation with her? About what she was planning?"

"Maybe. It wouldn't be pleasant, but I could go to the police down there and tell them about it. Still, I know I wasn't the only one she told. She mentioned it to Miss Gene and surely she shared the same information with her friends, or even her mother. I'm sure the police already know all about that. It's not really enough to charge him, much less convict him."

"Wouldn't it give them enough to bring him in?"

"Not to arrest him, no. They could talk to him, of course, but I don't see Jim Lazenby submitting himself to a real interrogation. He'd just call his lawyer, refuse to talk, and walk out on them." I sighed, "No, I don't think my talking to them would help that much. And I'd rather not admit to finding her body. If I did that, I could end up charged with obstruction."

We both declined dessert. With the martini and a glass of wine, I was feeling just a tiny bit loose. We left the restaurant for my house and coffee.

But somehow coffee turned into beer (I didn't have anything else to offer him) and one thing led, as these things do, to another. A little later we were once again wrapped around each other, lips and hands working busily.

There were only two things different from the last time we'd been in this situation. We were on my sofa instead of Nick's and, tonight, we didn't stop after kissing.

Later I couldn't decide just how it happened. One minute we were on the sofa, the next we were making our way into the bedroom, shedding clothes as we went.

In the past, I'd worried that sex with someone other than Owen would be awkward, but that thought didn't even enter my mind as Nick and I climbed beneath the covers and embraced each other from head to foot. Except for a bit of relief that I'd shaved my legs that morning, I didn't think of much of anything for the next couple of hours.

THIRTY-FIVE

I WOKE JUST BEFORE 8:00 TO THE SMELL OF COFFEE AND THE sound of someone moving things around in the kitchen—my kitchen. As the memory of the night before washed over me, my mind was full of equal parts of delight and concern. Delight because—well, that much should be obvious.

But the concern was real, too. How would Nick and I behave with each other after such intimacy? Would he be uncomfortable, eager to leave? And how would he rate the night before? How had I measured up to his expectations?

I pulled on jeans and a T-shirt and brushed my teeth, washed my face, and brushed my hair. Most Sundays I didn't bother with makeup, but most Sundays I wasn't sharing my house with a man, so I spent an extra few minutes with shadow and mascara, then took a steadying breath and went to greet the day—and Nick.

"Good morning, sunshine." He was standing in the kitchen and lifted a cup in my direction. "Want some coffee?"

"Oh, yes, please."

When I was close to him, he put two fingers under my chin, lifted my face, and planted a sweet kiss on my lips. "You're just as beautiful in the morning as you were last night."

I smiled at the flattery, but didn't mind it. "You don't look so bad yourself."

He ran a hand over his jaw. "A little scruffy, but a shave will take care of that." He sipped coffee. "I fed the cat—found his food in the pantry."

Curtis's bowl was empty, so I knew he'd eaten and was sleeping it off somewhere.

"Then I guess I'd better get busy and feed us."

We ate eggs, bacon, and biscuits at the small table in the kitchen. The biscuits were of the frozen variety—I don't see the point of putting all that time and effort into something that isn't going to be any better than what I can buy in the grocery store. But I did cook the eggs and bacon myself.

Surprisingly, there was no awkwardness between us, no nervous laughter or uncomfortable silences. I was more at ease with this man I'd known only a few weeks than I'd been with anyone in years.

He left before noon, although I wouldn't have minded if he'd stayed longer.

"Promised my son and his family I'd come to dinner today," he said. Then, with a grin, asked, "You want to come with me? They'd love you and you'll meet the whole family soon enough."

I took a deep breath. "No, I don't think so. It might be just a tiny bit too soon."

"It'll keep."

Before he left, we decided to get together the next night at his place.

"Nothing special," he said. "Maybe just TV and some popcorn."

I told him I'd be there at 7:00. "Popcorn sounds good." But we both knew what the main item on the menu would be.

I met Linda for lunch around 1:00. I wasn't especially hungry after the breakfast I'd had, so I just nibbled on a salad. Before we were halfway through the meal, she brought up the subject of the gun again.

"Can we go shoot this afternoon?"

"No, sorry, Linda. I'm beat from the trip." And from the night before, but I didn't mention that. "Maybe one day next week. Okay?"

"Okay. I just hope I don't need the gun before that."

I didn't even want to think about what might lead her to believe she needed it. "I thought you were going to get rid of it, Linda. I thought it scared you."

She chewed thoughtfully for a minute. "Yeah, but I think I'm more scared of somebody breaking in on me. If I practice enough, I can probably get used to the gun, don't you think?"

"Maybe so," I said without conviction. "But if you're determined, we'll try it again."

I spent the afternoon in pleasant laziness, reading bits and pieces of the Sunday paper while the Falcons did their thing on the television in the background. The only thing Nick had left behind was the occasional silly grin I found on my face from time to time.

Around 5:00, I called Miss Gene, feeling guilty that I hadn't done so before. The guilt increased when I had to listen to her tell me about Cheryl Pressley's murder and pretend I didn't know.

"It's such a shame," she said finally. "She was really a sweet girl. Everybody thinks it was Jim Lazenby, but nobody can prove it. I can't believe that man's gotten away with two murders and just goes on like everything's fine."

"At least we were able to get the Coopers' money back."

I told her everything that had happened on Friday and, by the time I finished, she was laughing.

"Oh, my. Oh, my. What I'd have given to see Jim Lazenby's face when you took that money from him. He's so greedy I think he'd rather give up an arm than $10,000. Oh, honey, you just made my day!"

I swore her to secrecy and promised to call again soon.

It was quarter to eight and I was contemplating changing into PJs and getting into bed with a new Mary Kay Andrews novel I'd picked up the day before when the phone rang.

"There's somebody in my house!"

"What? Linda, is that you?"

"Yes," she hissed. "You've got to come over right now. I'm standing in front of the house, but they could leave any time. What if they see me?"

I was on my feet, slipping into shoes. "Are you sure somebody's in there?"

"I know they are. I *heard* them, Emily! When I walked in the door tonight, something crashed somewhere. Just come — now! And bring your gun! Mine's in the house."

"Have you called the police?"

"Not yet. You're closer."

There was absolutely no logic to that, but this wasn't the time to argue. Feeling slightly ridiculous, I slipped the gun into the pocket of my jeans. Knowing Linda, she'd want to see it when I got there.

"Well, call them *now*. I'm on my way." I let myself out the front door, taking an extra three seconds to lock it behind me.

"No, stay on the phone with me, Emily. Please. I'll call them when you get here. I don't want you to hang up. You make me feel safe."

Ahh, more logic.

With my cell plastered to my ear, I trotted a block down the hill. Linda was standing on the sidewalk, wrapped in a dark wool cape.

"Thank God you're here! There really is somebody in there, Emily!"

There were no lights on in her house. "Did you just get home?"

She nodded. "I was down at the clubhouse—it's Mexican Train dominoes night, you know. Libby drove me home. As soon as I opened the back door I knew something was wrong. The whole atmosphere of the house was strange, negative somehow."

"You didn't call me down here just because the house felt negative, did you?" A gust of wind reminded me that it was now December.

"No, no. There was a sound—kind of a muffled crash—from somewhere in the house. The front bedroom, maybe. I didn't stay long enough to check it. Just ran back out here and called you." She looked at the phone in her hand. "Do you want me to call the police now?"

There hadn't been any sign of life from the house—no lights, no sound, no movement. "Not just yet. Did you see any sign of a break-in?"

"Ummmm...no...no break-in."

"Oh, Linda, you didn't leave the door unlocked?"

"Only the back door—the one to the patio. I was only gone for an hour or two. And I hate having to drag around a purse just for my keys. But when I got home the door was open—just a little."

I sighed. It was foolish to leave the house open, we both knew it, but I still didn't think there was an intruder in Linda's house—at least not a human intruder.

"Maybe there's a squirrel in your attic. That could have made the noise."

"It didn't sound like any squirrel I ever saw."

The wind blew her long hair away from her face. "It's chilly out here. Why don't we just go in and check?" I asked. "I'm sure there's a simple explanation…"

"I'm not setting foot inside that place until I know it's safe. I'll just call the police right now." Her voice was as hard as steel. For such a sweet little thing, she had always had a stubborn streak.

I put a hand on her arm. "Just hold on a minute. Let me go in and check it out."

I started up the short driveway.

"Yell if you want me to call the cops!"

I just nodded and kept walking. The sooner I found the squirrel, the quicker I could get back to Mary Kay Andrews. The walk around the house was a quick one—there are no large yards in Marchpoint—and I saw the sliding patio door was standing open, no doubt the way Linda left it when she ran out.

I honestly didn't believe there was anyone in the house, but habit and training kicked in as soon as I stepped inside. I moved quietly, feeling for the light switch. One click and the whole living room/dining room was bathed in light. Nothing seemed to be out of place. I turned on another light in the kitchen. Nothing there. The front bedroom, bathroom, and study all yielded the same result.

But the time I entered the master bedroom, I was convinced this whole thing had been the result of my friend's over-active imagination. The only exceptional thing about the master bath was the incredible number of exotic-looking herbal products Linda had lined up on the vanity.

I switched on the light and took a few steps into the adjacent walk-in closet. None of her clothes or shoes seemed disturbed. I'd left the closet and returned to the bedroom before it registered… something was not quite right. As quietly as I could, I went back. My eyes made a slow circuit of the closet. Then I saw it.

At the far end, I could see two pale blue shoe covers. Peeking out from behind a bunch of long dresses, they were made of paper and had elastic tops. I looked closer. Above the elastic tops were a couple of inches of pale legs.

I was so astonished that, for a second, I just stood there and gaped. Then common sense prevailed.

I pulled the gun from my pocket, suddenly grateful I'd brought it along, and pointed it at the blue feet.

"Come out of there right now or I'll shoot you where you stand!" When that provoked no movement, I said. "Now! Move it!"

The dresses kind of rippled, then the clothing parted, and the burglar stepped out of his hiding place, ducking his head to clear the clothes rod.

I don't know if I was more shocked by the fact that the intruder was Milton Overton or that, except for the shoe covers and a shower cap, he was stark naked. Extremely naked, in fact. Before I could avert my eyes, I noticed that his pubic area had been shaved clean. He had no weapon, just a plastic shopping bag in his right hand.

"What the *hell* are you doing here?"

He didn't answer.

"Put the bag down and move away from it," I told him. He did so. "Now come out here and go stand by the toilet."

He did as I asked and I glanced into the bag on the floor. I could see a bottle of wine and what looked like a tangle of jewelry. "*You're the thief?*"

For a long moment we just stood there, me holding a gun and Milton, ashamed and naked, unable to meet my eyes. It was just as well. I couldn't stand that sight any longer. I grabbed a bright orange and pink robe from a hook on the back of the door.

"Put that on."

He pulled on the silken garment and tied the sash. He was a small man. Even though it was tight across his back, the robe covered what it needed to.

"Let's go."

We walked out the front door to the sidewalk, Milton leading the way. The robe made faint swishing noises as he walked. I followed, gun still in my hand. I probably didn't need it, probably hadn't needed it since I walked in the door, but I wasn't going to put it away until he was in custody. I didn't really think Milton was dangerous, but I was pretty sure he was crazy as a loon. Who knew what he might do?

Linda's eyes widened to comic proportions when she saw us.

"Call the police," I told her.

"I ... uh ..." She was having a hard time keeping her eyes off Overton. "I already did ... when you were in there so long. I knew something was wrong."

I nodded. "Well, here's the neighborhood thief."

"Yeah," she said. "Why did you make him dress up in my robe?"

"I had to have something to cover him up. He was naked."

"Ewww. And you used my silk robe? Now I'll have to burn it."

The patrol car was there in less than five minutes. Unlike the television shows, the officer arrived quietly. There were no lights and sirens to bring out the neighbors.

The officer was a veteran with graying hair and a patient attitude. His name tag identified him as J.R. Miller. He did a double take when he saw Milton, but calmly asked what was going on.

I quickly related what had happened and Linda told him how terrified she'd been — at least five times. Milton never said a word. Once Miller heard our story, he put Milton, still in the robe, in the back of his car.

"You said he had a bag of stuff he was stealing?"

I led the way back into the house to the closet where I pointed to the plastic bag. "He was holding that."

He picked it up, looked inside, then held it out to Linda. "Do you recognize these things?"

"The wine's mine, of course and that's my mother's necklace." She reached into the bag. "And my wedding ring! That nasty little son of a bitch was going to steal my wedding ring!"

After getting our names and other information, Officer Miller was ready to go.

"I guess you know that there's been a number of thefts in your neighborhood," he said. "This'll probably clear a lot of cases." He opened the driver's door. "There'll be detectives following up on this. They'll get your jewelry and robe back to you."

"Thanks, but I don't want the robe back. Milton can keep it."

THIRTY-SIX

THE NEXT WEEK SEEMED TO FLY BY. I WAS ASSIGNED TO SEV-
eral new cases at the DA's office and my evenings, or most of them
anyway, were happily occupied with Nick Buckley.

On Tuesday, I met with two detectives from the Blount County
Police Department. They ask me a few more questions, but were
clearly in wrap-up mode. Milton Overton had confessed to all the
burglaries that had been reported in Marchpoint Manse in the last
two months.

"Hell, we couldn't shut him up," one told me. "He wanted to tell
us all about it. Seemed to think he was providing a service, showing
people how lax they'd become, leaving their doors unlocked and
valuables laying around."

"Yeah," his partner said. "He never did anything with the stuff
he took—had it all piled in the corner of his garage."

I asked the question that was on everybody's mind. "Why in the
world was he naked."

The first detective grinned. "Television. Seems that Milton really loves those police shows—you know, the ones where the crime
scene techs solve all the murders and the lazy detectives don't do
anything?"

I smiled. "Yep. I know the ones you mean."

"Well, anyhow, Milton made up his mind he wasn't going to get caught by any of that forensic stuff. So, when he was going to burglarize a house, he'd take off all his clothes and leave them nearby—usually in the woods behind the houses. As he explained it, he didn't want to take a chance that he'd leave any kind of trace evidence behind. Same thing with the hairnet and shoe covers and," he grinned, "the shaving. Didn't want to take a chance on some forensic genius finding a stray hair. He'd only wear the net and covers once, then throw them away. Had a whole box of both."

"But what about other hairs? I mean, there's chest and armpits and..."

"Shaved."

"Huh?"

"He shaved his whole body smooth as a baby's butt. Like one of those Olympic swimmers, you know? They shave to cut down resistance in the water."

I was having a hard time processing everything they were telling me. How could we have lived around someone that over the edge and not recognized it?

"What was it?" I asked. "Does he have Alzheimer's or something?"

"Don't think so. He doesn't seem to have any cognitive problems."

"No," the second man said. "He's just crazy as a shithouse rat." He smiled. "At least that's my professional opinion."

Wednesday afternoon, Annette and I spent two hours prepping for an upcoming robbery trial. And she invited me to dinner at her place Saturday night.

"There's someone special I want you to meet."

"Really?"

"Ummhmm. His name is Scott."

"I can't wait."

She smiled like a happy cat. "You'll love him. I know you will. Oh, and you can bring somebody, if you want."

I told her I thought I would.

So Saturday night Nick and I spent a pleasant four hours in Annette's loft. She greeted Nick like an old friend. Dinner was delicious and the company just fine. As she predicted, I did like Scott. He was charming, entertaining and, best of all, clearly adored my friend.

The conversation ranged from the dangerous to the nutty—our adventures in Fitzgerald to Milton Overton. Spirits were high and there was a lot of laughter. The only unhappy note that evening was the subject of Cheryl Pressley.

"It's so sad. She was convinced she had everything under control," I said.

"I don't understand why she kept that recording at her house," Annette said. "It was such a dangerous thing to do."

"Yeah," Scott agreed. "Why not make a copy and give it to a lawyer or somebody. That way she'd have had some insurance."

I almost dropped my beer. "Maybe she did," I said slowly. "I think she might have done just that."

I went to find my purse. As I was scrabbling around to find my phone, I told the others, "I have to make a call."

I found the number I wanted on a scrap of paper and dialed. She answered on the fifth ring.

"Miss Gene, it's Emily Christopher. I apologize for calling so late."

"Oh, it's not late, honey. It's not even eleven yet. I never go to bed before midnight. So how are you doing?"

"I'm fine, Miss Gene. But I need to ask you a favor."

"Sure, honey, whatever I can do."

"You know that frog that Cheryl Pressley gave you?"

"Oh, yes. I can see it from where I'm sitting."

"Could you look at it real close and see if there could be something hidden inside? A note or something like that?"

"I can. Let me just put the phone down for a minute."

I stood there while Miss Gene went to check the frog. The others were silent, watching me as I waited.

After what seemed like a long time, Miss Gene was back. "I don't know how you knew it, but there is something inside. I can't tell what it is, but I can see something through the little hole in the bottom. And, you know, now that I look at this frog close-up, it looks like it might have been broken at one time, then glued back together."

My heart was beating fast now. "Would you ... I hate to ask, but it's really important. Could you break open that frog and see what's inside?"

She hesitated a few seconds, then said, "I'll do my best. Putting the phone down again."

I listened to her movements for a minute or two, then heard two thuds.

"Well, I'll be dogged," she said when she came back to the phone. "I don't know how you knew it, but there was a tiny little thing inside. I think it's one of those things you plug into your computer. What do they call it? Is it memory stick?"

"That's exactly what they call it," I said.

"I hope I didn't hurt it getting the frog open; had to use a hammer to break it. I've never used one of these, but I've got my computer right here. Should I try to see if I can plug it in?"

"No!" I said, scared to death the device could be damaged somehow. I thought for a second. "Tell you what. I'll drive down in the morning. I need to talk to the police anyway. We'll take it to them then. It just might be what they need to prove what happened to Cheryl Pressley."

"Oh, I hope so. And I'd love to see you again."

"Just don't tell anybody that you have it."

I ended the call, then told Annette, Scott, and Nick about the side of the conversation they hadn't heard.

"You know there's got to be something good on that thumb drive," Annette said, "or Cheryl wouldn't have hidden it like that."

"We'll see. I'm going down tomorrow and meet with Miss Gene. We'll take the thumb drive to the police and I'll tell them about my conversation with Cheryl. Maybe it will be enough. Just depends on what's on the recording." I looked at Annette. "You've been in this thing since the beginning. You want to go with me?"

"I can't. Scott and I are driving over to Birmingham." She reached across the corner of the table and squeezed his hand. "I want him to meet my mother."

Scott smiled like he'd won the lottery.

"I'll go," Nick said. "Maybe I can keep you out of trouble."

THIRTY-SEVEN

NICK DROVE US TO FITZGERALD. HE'D OFFERED TO TAKE THE Harley, but I'd refused. Clinging to him on the back of a motorcycle for several cold hours wasn't my idea of fun. We headed south in his comfy red Lexus. It made my sedate CR-V look like some grandmother's car—which, now that I thought about it, it was.

The day was cool and bright and, as we drove south, the autumn colors, which had already peaked in our section of the state, became more vibrant.

"I'm finally going to get to meet your witch," he said. "Do you think she'll make me a potion or something."

I looked over at his handsome face. "I think she'll make you whatever you want. What is it you need?"

"I wouldn't mind some kind of love charm." He smiled at me. "You know, something to keep you close by."

"Don't think you're going to need a charm for that." I put a hand on his arm. "I'm not going anywhere."

"Good to hear."

We pulled into Miss Gene's gravel drive just after 1:00. She was out on the porch before the car came to a stop.

"I'm so glad you're here," she said, giving me a hug. "I've been worried all night with that thing in my house, scared Jim Lazenby might know about it somehow and try to come and get it."

"It'll be gone soon," I told her. "This is my friend Nick Buckley, Miss Gene."

She put out a thin, veined hand. "Nice to meet you."

"It's a pleasure, Miss Gene. Emily told me what a great help you've been."

She gave me a smile. "Well, come on in. The wind's got a little bite to it today."

We followed her into the house where a small fire burned in the fireplace. The cat slept on the hearth and didn't even open an eye at our entrance.

"Can I offer you a cup of coffee or maybe a glass of tea?"

"No, thanks," I told her. "I think we better get on down to the police department."

"We'll have to go to the sheriff's office," Miss Gene said. "City police are only responsible for what happens inside the city limits. Cheryl lived in the county."

I nodded. "Well, wherever we're going, we should probably go now. This is Sunday and there's no telling how long it'll take them to get in touch with one of the people working the Pressley case."

Miss Gene stepped into the kitchen and we followed. She opened the oven on her ancient stove and took out a brown paper bag. "Thought this would be the best hiding place. That little doo-dad's in here, along with the pieces of the frog that I broke. The police might want to see that, too."

"Good thinking," Nick said.

She banked the fire and put a wire screen on the hearth. Then we all went out the door. Miss Gene climbed into the back of Nick's car and we bounced back down the drive.

The Ben Hill County Sheriff's Department was located in an industrial area south of town. We parked in the nearly empty visitors lot and went in.

The deputy behind the glassed-in counter wore a crisp khaki-colored uniform. He looked like he wasn't many years out of the academy. He listened politely when I asked to speak with one of the investigators on the Cheryl Pressley case.

"Well now, that's Markham and Coley. I don't believe either one of them is working today. They'll be in tomorrow. You could come back then or you can talk to the investigator on duty. That'd be Bill McGraw."

"We'd rather talk with the guys working the case," I explained. "We've got some information that may be important."

"It's Sunday, ma'am, and if it's not an emergency, I'm not calling them in. Detective McGraw can take the information from you and make sure it gets to the right place..."

Miss Gene stepped around me to peer through the window. "Now, Danny Nicholls, you ought to know it's important if I came down here myself on a Sunday."

He swallowed hard. "Oh, yes, ma'am, Miss Gene, but they don't like it if we bother people at home when they're off..."

"And *I* don't like getting the runaround when I'm trying to share some information that might just put a murderer in jail. Now you call one of those fellas—Markham or—did you say Coley? Is that Larry Coley?"

"Yes, ma'am, *Detective* Coley."

"Well, you call one of them right now so we can get this over with."

Nicholls swallowed hard. "Yes, ma'am. I'll call—but I can't promise they'll come in. After all, it is Sunday."

Miss Gene turned away from the window, walked across the room and sat down, feet together and back as straight as a board. Nick and I followed. Her face was set in a serious frown, but there was a twinkle in her eye when she nodded toward the deputy and whispered to me, "Larry's mama comes to see me regular."

Fifty minutes later, Investigator L.R. Coley walked into the lobby. He was a tall, red-haired man of about 50 and he didn't look happy to be there. After introductions, he took us to a conference room in the back of the building.

"Okay," he said. "What's this all about?"

"Are you working the Cheryl Pressley murder?" I asked.

"Yeah," he said impatiently. "Why?"

"I talked to Cheryl a week or two before she was killed and she told me that she had a recording of some kind and that Jim Lazenby was going to pay big, that her baby would have everything it ever wanted. She said the recording could send him to jail for a long time."

"She told me the same thing, near enough," Gene said.

Coley had been slowly nodding as I told my story. "Yeah, she told you and she told you, Miss Gene, and damn near anybody else in town that would listen. This isn't exactly new information."

"But we have the recording," Miss Gene told him. That definitely got Coley's attention.

Miss Gene carefully removed the thumb drive and the pieces of the broken purple frog from the bag and laid them on the wood surface of the table. "She brought me that frog a while back. And that little stick thing was hid inside it." She picked it up in her hand. "Now we'll all see what's on it."

Coley reached out a hand to her. "I'll take that, Miss Gene."

"No, sir. We've all been through a lot and I won't give it to you unless you play it right here for all of us to hear."

That surprised me, but I hoped she'd win the battle of wills. I certainly wanted to hear what Cheryl had recorded.

Coley's lips tightened. "Ma'am, that may be evidence in a murder investigation. I have every right to take it. Now if you'll just..."

"It's my property until a judge says different. Do you want to take the time to try and find a judge that sees it your way, Larry, or do you want to play it here and now and maybe get on with arresting the man who killed Cheryl Pressley? If not, I'll walk right out of here with it."

His eyes went from her face to the thumb drive and back to her face. Evidently, he realized that her expression left no doubt she meant every word she said. It was clear he didn't want to get into a physical struggle with the witch.

He huffed out a breath. "Okay. Give it here. I'll play it for you."

But she didn't hand it over. "Ummmm...I don't think so, Larry. Once you get it in your hand, you might just take it away." She looked at me. "Do you know how to get this thing to play, honey?"

"Yes, ma'am," I told her. "I do." I glanced at Coley. "We'll need a laptop or a tablet."

He stared at me for a minute, then gave a quick nod. "I'll be right back."

He was back in less than a minute with a slim laptop. He opened it, pushed a button and, a few seconds later, the screen lit up.

Miss Gene gave me, not Coley, the thumb drive. I pushed it into a USB port and, when it came up on the screen, found the right button and pushed it. Everyone was quiet, straining to listen.

There were some muffled bumps, then a man's voice which I assumed was Lazenby's.

"What are you doing over there?"

There was a slight slur to his voice and I wondered how much he'd had to drink.

"Just getting me a breath mint, sugar." I recognized Cheryl Pressley's voice. *"Want to be sweet for my man."*

"You really want to be sweet, you'll go get me another drink."

"I can do that." I thought I heard a smile in her voice.

We sat through thirty seconds or so of silence, only hearing the hiss of the recorder and vague sounds of background movement. Then Cheryl spoke again.

"Here you go, baby. I made it a double, just like you like it."

There was the sound of tinkling of ice and a faint slurp. *"Oh, yeah. Just what I needed."* He chuckled. *"I rang your bell good that time, didn't I, baby?"*

"You always do, Jimmy." We could hear some rustling and I imagined her snuggling up to him under the covers. *"You catch your breath and you can do it again."*

He laughed. *"You're goddamned right I will! We got some shit to celebrate tonight."* The slur was more pronounced now.

Cheryl gave a little laugh. *"I guess we do. I 'bout fainted when I opened that letter and found that check! Two million dollars for Mr. Eckley's dying!"*

I realized the recording had been made several years ago when Lazenby got the insurance check for Eckley's death.

More ice rattling. *"Yeah. Nice. Real nice."*

"I don't mean to say I'm not sorry Mr. Eckley got killed—that was awful—but at least you got the insurance money and you can pay off

all those bills. I was really worried for a while that you were... well, going to go bankrupt or something. It's terrible to say, but you were really lucky, Jim."

"Luck had nothing to do with it, baby. A man like me makes his own luck."

"What do you mean?"

Cheryl's voice was just the right mixture of awe and wonder. It sounded like

he gulped more of the drink. *"I mean that Eckley didn't run into a deer. He ran into Royal."*

"Royal Van Zandt? I don't understand, sugar."

"Royal owed me a favor." Another chuckle. *"Hell, Royal owes me a lot of goddamn favors. He took care of Eckley. I mean—we were going to lose everything. The only way to fix it was one of us had to go and it sure as hell wasn't going to be me!"*

"You mean Royal killed him in that wreck?"

"Well, he tried. But Royal ain't no goddamn genius. He didn't get the job done running him off the road. Had to finish it with a baseball bat. Incompetent asshole. But it was okay. Cops were happy to write it off as an accident." More ice rattled. *"Hey, go get me another drink. Then we got us some unfinished business to tend to."*

"Okay, sugar." More rustling of bedcovers. *"And I need another breath..."*

The recording stopped and we sat in shocked silence for a minute.

"For someone who is supposed to be so sharp," Nick said, "that was particularly stupid. Why would tell her all that?"

Miss Gene just shook her head. "He never thought she'd say anything. Besides, who'd believe her? It would be the word of a pillar of the community against a receptionist. An unemployed receptionist, at that, the second she opened her mouth."

Coley nodded.

"Who's Royal Van Zandt?" I asked, remembering the man who'd come after me with a bat.

Miss Gene sniffed indignantly. "He's from over in Crisp County—never been any good. In and out of prison just like his brothers. He'd do 'bout anything for a few hundred dollars, which I'm sure Jim Lazenby was happy to give him." She turned her attention to Coley. "So what now?"

"Now we take your statement, Miss Gene." He looked at Nick and me. "If you wouldn't mind waiting in the lobby?"

It took more than an hour for Coley to get Miss Gene's statement. Nick and I spent most of our time walking around the parking lot where we could speak freely.

"I guess that'll do it for Lazenby," Nick said.

"Maybe. That recording might not even be admissible evidence. I'm thinking the key will be Royal Van Zandt. They'll pick him up, of course. A lot will depend on what he tells them."

"Do you think he'll talk?"

I shrugged. "Don't know. If that bat's still in his truck, he's toast. Whether he's washed it or not, there'll probably still be trace evidence on it to connect him to Eckley. And he's been in the system before. He'll know his best chance will be giving them Lazenby. It'll be the difference between a death sentence and life in prison."

It was getting dark when we drove Miss Gene back to her house. Nick waited in the car while I walked with her to the door.

"I don't know how to thank you for all you've done," I told her.

"Honey, you're the one did all the work. And look how it paid off. I'd bet my last nickel that Jim Lazenby will be in jail this time tomorrow."

"I hope you're right." I gave her a hug, handed her an envelope, and turned back to the car.

"What's this?"

"Just your share," I said. "I know you'll use it for something good."

I climbed into the car, then looked back. Miss Gene was standing on her porch waving goodbye.

We stopped at a Waffle House before we started home. Sometimes a patty melt with hash browns is the most satisfying meal ever.

THIRTY-EIGHT

I WAS BUSY THE NEXT WEEK, BUT SPOKE WITH MISS GENE three times. She had such good contacts in the community that I couldn't have gotten more complete information if Detective Coley had been giving me hourly bulletins on everything that happened.

"They arrested Royal Van Zandt Sunday night," she told me. "Just a few hours after we left the police station. I heard he started singing like a bird just as soon as they snapped those cuffs on his wrists. He confessed to killing poor Frankie Eckley and beating up a couple of other people that Lazenby was having trouble with.

"He even admitted running you off the road, honey. And he told them Jim Lazenby had paid him to do it." She giggled. "Danny Nicholls said if he'd thought it would help him, Royal would have given up his mother and the rest of his family, too."

"Did they find the baseball bat?"

"They sure did. Under the seat in his truck. The fool was too stupid to get rid of it. And from what I hear, they found some kind of evidence on it."

"Do they think it will be enough to get Lazenby, too?"

"Seems like it. I'll let you know."

Annette had given me four cases Monday morning and I spent much of the week working on them. Nick and I saw each other several times and, each time we were together, I was more sure about the relationship we were building.

Tuesday afternoon I was looking out my kitchen window when Owen's new wife, Sarah, came speed walking past my house, a grim look of concentration on her face. I waited for the anger to come, but it didn't and I realized I didn't care what she did or where she lived. She and Owen simply didn't matter to me anymore. I was smiling as I poured water into my cup for tea.

Friday morning, I took the files, investigations complete, back to Annette.

"They all check out," I told her, settling in a chair facing her desk. "You're good to go on them."

"Glad to hear that. Any word from Fitzgerald?"

I brought her up to date on the latest from Miss Gene concerning Royal Van Zandt's confession.

"They had him cold," I said, "with his confession and the bat, but the icing on the cake was when Royal produced two notes from Lazenby. On one was a description of my vehicle, complete with tag number. On the other was Eckley's name, a description of *his* car and the location on Ten Mile Road where, presumably, Royal was supposed to find him. They're both in Lazenby's handwriting."

Annette was nodding in appreciation. "Who'd have expected Van Zandt to be smart enough to keep those?"

"Guess he wasn't as stupid as Lazenby thought. Miss Gene heard he told the police he kept them for insurance. Guess it paid off."

"What about Lazenby?"

"They picked him up Wednesday morning, marched him right out of his office in handcuffs for the whole town to see."

Annette had a big smile on her face. "The pillar of the community! Lord, I wish I could have seen that. It would have done me good to watch that condescending bastard being brought down. Oh, well, maybe I'll drive down for his trial—just to watch him squirm in the defendant's chair."

"No, you won't. There's not going to be a trial."

"Why?"

I delivered my best piece of news. "The Ben Hill County DA made it clear that, if they had to go to trial, he'd be asking for the death penalty. And after the police and his attorney explained the facts of life to him, Lazenby decided not to give a jury a shot at him."

"Probably a wise decision, considering how many people he's screwed over in that town. You know at least a few of their friends or relatives would be on the jury."

"Ummmhmmm," I said, "bound to be. And Lazenby had to know that. He confessed to paying Royal Van Zandt to kill Eckley and me. He's going to plead to murder and attempted murder in exchange for a life sentence with the possibility of parole."

"What about Cheryl Pressley?"

I shook my head. "That's the bad news. He wouldn't come across on Cheryl and they don't have enough evidence to be sure of a conviction."

"I hate that," Annette said. "There ought to be justice for Cheryl."

"Yeah, I know, but I guess he'll be punished for her murder along with the one he's pleading to."

Annette changed the subject. "What'd you do with your share of the money?"

"Gave it to Miss Gene. You?"

"Humane Society."

In late February, Annette and I drove back to Fitzgerald. We were in the courtroom when Jim Lazenby stood before a superior court judge and entered guilty pleas to all charges. Robyn Lazenby was nowhere to be seen, although his son and daughter were sitting right behind him.

The judge didn't waste time lecturing him. He simply followed the prosecution's recommendation and sentenced Lazenby to life with the possibility of parole. I hated the idea he might be out of prison someday, but understood why the DA went along with the plea. You never knew what a jury might do.

When the deputies led him away, Lazenby didnt even glance at anyone else, his whole attention was focused inward. It was a fitting way for him to leave, since that was the way he'd lived his whole life.

Before leaving Ben Hill County, we drove out to Imogene Crump's house and gave her a tiny jeweled frog I'd found in a shop up in Helen where Nick and I had spent the New Year's weekend. Then we headed home.

CPSIA information can be obtained
at www.ICGtesting.com
Printed in the USA
FFOW03n2251130917
39927FF